Rescuing Tinku

The Story of
Major Raj Pratap Singh

Also by Vaneeta Vaid

9789380502939
₹ 195.00
102 pp | PB | 2012

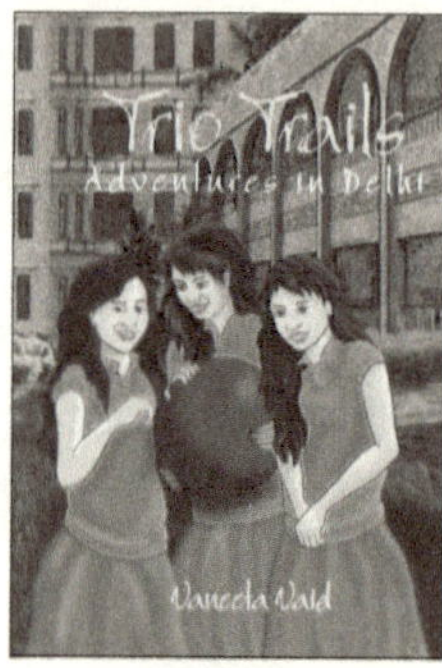

9789380502946
₹ 175.00
80 pp | PB | 2012

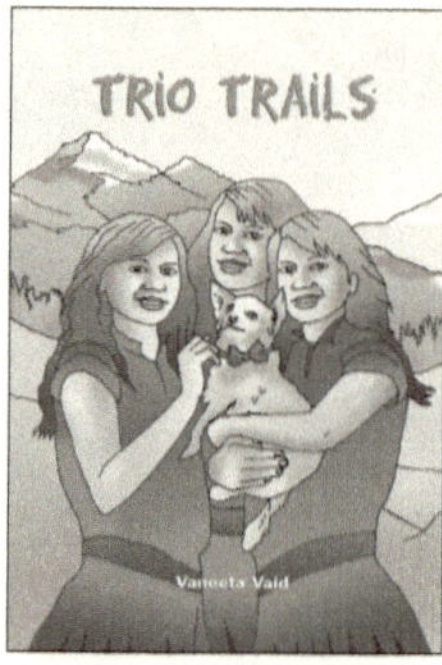

9788187966968
₹ 145.00
118 pp | PB | 2009

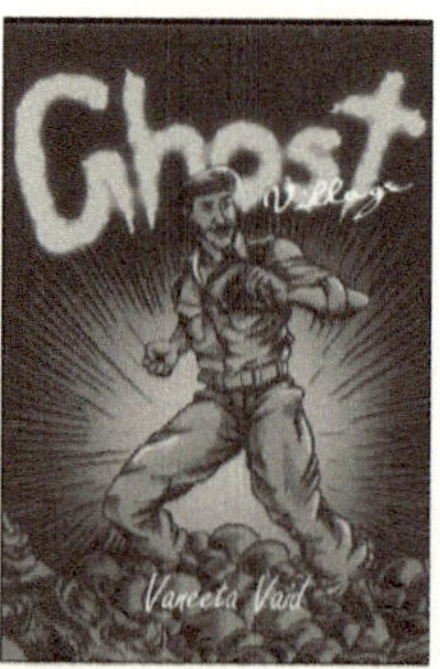

9789380502892
₹ 195.00
80 pp | PB | 2012

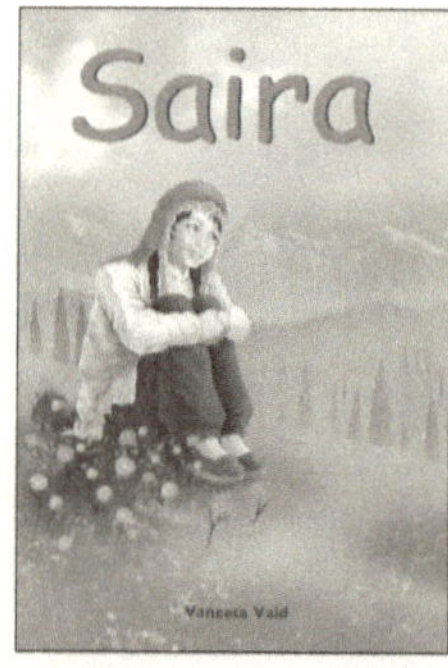

9788187966623
₹ 165.00
136 pp | PB | 2008

8187966424
₹ 75.00
78 pp | PB | 2005

Rescuing Tinku

The Story of
Major Raj Pratap Singh

VANEETA VAID

KW Publishers Pvt Ltd
New Delhi

In association with

Integrated Capital Services Ltd.
www.raas.co.in

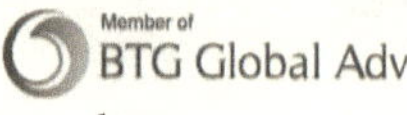

Member of
BTG Global Advisory
www.btgga.com

ISBN   978-93-86288-79-0   Paperback
ISBN   978-93-86288-80-6   ebook

Published in India by Kalpana Shukla

KW Publishers Pvt Ltd
4676/21, First Floor, Ansari Road
Daryaganj, New Delhi 110002
Phone: +91 11 23263498/43528107
Marketing: knowledgeworld@kwpub.com
Editorial: jose@kwpub.com
Website: www.kwpub.com

Printed and Bound in India.

*Dedicated to the
Soldiers of the Indian Armed Forces,
who tirelessly guard our borders
and keep us safe.*

Major Raj Pratap Singh

Major Raj Pratap Singh signaled with his eyes to his colleagues to be absolutely still. They complied. Slowly-very slowly Raj picked up his binoculars, as did the others, and peered through them. Unwittingly a slow sigh of wonderment escaped their lips in chorus!

Up beyond lingered the magnificent tiger. Observing the splendid tiger, so unaware of any dangers, Raj felt his heart lurch; only because he remembered that due to human apathy this animal was on the verge of extinction. We all know tigers are now considered to be endangered. Sadly they are hunted and killed for their pelt, nails and other superstitious beliefs. He never wanted to imagine a world without this beautiful animal. Even as he gazed with his colleagues, the tiger seemed to be completely unaware of the intrusion of his peace by the humans. Pawing into the air and rolling with some inner joy-yes totally unaware!!! The tiger did not rejoice because his stripes beautifully glinted in the dew covered morning sunlight or that his huge jaw and massive paws made him one of the most majestic creatures hereabouts-*he was just so happy*! His onlookers would never know why- but his delight seemed catching, since they all watched with slow smiles forming around their lips!

Some distance away, a green Army gypsy jeep stood. Raj and two other fellow officers were off the very same jeep, crouched by the shrubs allowing the tiger his privacy. The gypsy driver too crouched behind them. Even as they watched, the tiger rose. He yawned; lazily stretched and then with an indifferent flick of his tail walked impressively on-deeper into the jungle.

"He is well fed....not hunting I can see!" Raj intoned very softly, adding, "do you think he knew we were watching and benevolently let us be, he, being benevolent because he had a satisfying meal hmm???

Captain Prakash heard him, even though Raj spoke in a low voice. He smiled and whispered back, "yes thankfully he was

not hungry or attacking sir, I would hate to be chased by that apparently humungous mammal!"

That brought a chuckle from everyone; as they observed the tiger going into the folds of a thick woody patch, out of sight.

"Whew" came a collective sigh from those present, as the tiger completely disappeared into the thick jungle vegetation.

"Now that was some show "ol" tiger put up!" Laughed Captain Jones!

"I know-he was so er...*happy!*" interjected Prakash.

Silently they moved towards the vehicles, still quite enthralled by the recent events.

Raj broke into the silence with, "Let us go! We have to clear this place by sunset. Also...!"

He was interrupted by a grind of brakes and gears as two Army gypsy jeeps frenetically raced into the clearing where they were!

These vehicles that had just arrived were with Raj's group. They had somehow lagged behind, arriving in a flurry just now.

"SSSSSSSSSH!" Raj in some amusement

kept a finger on his lips towards the Junior Commissioned Officer, (JCO). The JCO sprang from the Jeep and came to him. "Silence please, there is a tiger in the vicinity. He just left-but we do not want *him* to *get too curious and return!*" Raj jocularly commented to the JCO.

The JCO smiled in confusion at Raj's comment, adding his own explanation for his delay alongside.

"Sir your Gypsy raced ahead-we—er—ran into a persistent Rhino, plumb in the middle of the track refusing to budge ... he finally did move and... !"

"No problem Saab! We did get a little heady with the speed. However we managed to spot a tiger, as I was saying...!" Raj went on to relate their recent experience.

Raj had joined his battalion, which was posted to the borders of the state of Arunachal Pradesh and Assam.

These borders of Northeast were extremely sensitive areas. Threat from beyond was there, but the threat within the state was very evident too. Extortion, kidnapping and terror disturbed peace in these environs more than often! Arunachal Pradesh borders the states of Assam and Nagaland to the south, and shares international borders with Burma in the east, Bhutan in the west, and the People's Republic of China in the north. Arunachal Pradesh means "land of the dawn lit mountains" in Sanskrit. It is also known as "land of the rising sun" in reference to its position as the easternmost state of India. The sun rises very, very early here. Do you know day light is as early as 3 am? The reason being that the geography of these places put them in the Northeast and since the sun rises in the east they have the earliest daylight! Raj's battalion was at Arunachal Pradesh closer to the borders of Assam. The geography of their location put them right in between the lush tea gardens of Assam and rich wild life of Arunachal!

These states are rich in wild life! In fact Arunachal Pradesh is perhaps the only State which has four major cats, tiger, leopard , clouded leopard and snow leopard . Lesser cats like the golden cat, leopard cat and the marbled cat are also found here. But apart from the big cats here one could spot many types of birds, elephants, wild buffaloes also!

Here was a world that was so different from the usual city hustle and bustle that tempted so many; people who loved the city bright lights rather than live in the lap of such healthy natural environments! This place was bursting with greenery and vibrant energy that comes from the atmosphere being engulfed with jungles teeming with wild life and vegetation!

Tea gardens dotted entire landscapes. During spring and early May long lines of traditional tea pickers with baskets on their backs alongside rows and rows of tea bushes could be seen. Yes, the healthy outcome of fertile lands was evident. Lush greenery, abundant wildlife and heavy rainfalls marked characteristics here. Respect to the coming and goings of Elephants, Rhinos, Tigers, Leopards, was an imperative! Traffic was literally guided by the spotting of herds etc!

The small contingent drove out of the bumpy jungle tracks. This time they coordinated their pace together!

Raj sat in front. He kept his eyes alert as did everyone else as they moved further into the jungle tracks. Visually the apparent calmness provided by beautiful backdrop could be misleading. These areas were particularly susceptible to militant threat. The thick vegetation could be hiding some gun toting miscreants, which could lead to an unexpected ambush. Luckily nothing of that sort happened.

The 'kutcha' road threw their machines into a rattle. But they had to maintain a fast speed to quickly clear the jungle. They were returning from a routine patrol to the higher regions. These patrols were necessary to keep a pulse on what was happening around the borders. Their aim was to check into any untoward suspicious movements by the locals. These checkouts were efficient and well managed. Completely unobtrusive since the endeavor was not to alarm or harass the locals. Mostly the army was welcomed hereabouts since the soldiers brought medicine, rations and other succors for them. This happened because somewhere the villagers, through them, were discovering a life that was so different outside their own spheres. Hesitantly at first they shared their needs to the visiting forces and in turn willing

help came. Soon the demands were more frank. Somehow an acceptance for the men in olive green developed! Remember these areas were so remote that reaching them was an arduous task! However army patrols did do their rounds and now were familiar visitors! At first the villagers were very cold and unwelcoming. But over the years realizing that these men in green were there to protect the borders, *and even help* thawed them.

A famous story went around in this particular village when many years ago, Kinta the local hunter was ensnared by a deadly trap set for rabbits. Kinta was badly injured in the ankle and he came screaming to the local medicine man to give him something for the excruciating pain his wounds were causing him. No poultice or herbs helped. A rough splint with bamboos was affected too. Nothing helped. Then the local medicine man screamed and pointed at the raw, bleeding split skin and proclaimed that a spirit had entered the wound and was consuming Kinta through it. Screams and horror followed from the gullible villagers. At that point in time who could blame them? Steeped in their own superstitions and very much cut off from the world due to their geographical locations, their ignorance was not surprising.

Poor Kinta suddenly found himself kicked out of any orbit of concern! He became a taboo overnight. After a few days on a routine patrol an Army jeep crawled its way up to the village. The locals were still wary of them at that point. Seeing Kinta, all alone writhing under a tree the Captain heading the contingent was curious. His investigations led him to check the wound, promptly force Kinta to take a pain killer after something to eat. Fortunately a first aid kit is always carried on these trips by the soldiers. Within no time Kinta sat up. Relieved from the pain Kinta was so happy he readily went with the army persons back to the camp medical clinic. After some days, nicely stitched up and recovered, Kinta grandly returned. His heady stories about the camp and the life much, much below these environs, in the plains, invited a ready audience from the locals. He somehow became a hero! After this incident it is believed the locals were more welcoming to the patrols regular visits!

When Raj got posted here army patrols had become an acknowledged norm.

Raj and his men had spent at least two hours mingling with the motley of villagers in one of the remotest points of the borders today morning. Raj marveled at the simplicity of these village folks. So ensconced were they in their existence that cut them off completely from mainstream that they knew no other life! For them it was all about their livestock, tilling and the weather. In all this purity of routines, ugly misdoings of people with mean intentions marred the atmosphere. Raj hated to think at the reasons that brought him here. He mentally prayed that they would keep the ugliness away from this peaceful settlement! Initially he was also shocked at the local mumbo jumbo attached to medical treatments. Any illness here was treated with herbs plucked of trees. But interaction with them, other government bodies and of course the famous Kinta story, over the years saw a slow awareness of medicines. Just few months back an army doctor had visited them and given them a talk on hygiene. This intrusion of the doctor thrilled the locals! It was still a hot topic of conversation amongst them! "Saab tell us that if we keep washing our hands we will never be ill? That is what "dactor" Babu said??!" or "Is it true that in high fever we should bathe?"Over hot cups of tea Raj, Prakash and John tried to answer all the questions!

Now, just as they cleared the jungles, the route took on another stance! Landscapes swiftly changed. The continuity of thick flora that interrupted their paths before gave way to a proper road edged by different shrubbery and water bodies as they raced ahead.

Below a gushing waterfall pooling into a pond flanked the left side of the road. A tiny herd of elephants joyfully bathed under the fall. As the vehicles whizzed past, and Raj noticed the waterfall, he missed his camera. Carrying a camera for these operations was not feasible. However Raj loved to dapple in photography in his free time. Since his postings took him to these unbelievably striking places he had developed a passion for photography. Raj began to recollect how he had picked up his passion for photography. It was during his academy days that he had enrolled into the photography club. There he had the opportunity to single out everything there was to know about photography and cameras'.

For a very long time Raj had completely forgotten this hobby of his since he was busy with many other adventures. However coming to this beautiful location, juxtaposition with amazing wild life, he fished out his camera and decided to create a photo-album scrap book for himself. Raj reflected on his was posting to the Kashmir borders. There he was idly clicking with his digital camera. Later when he saw the photographs he realized that he had captured the sun casting a mottled streak of dazzling light over the towering, bare mountains surrounding the location. He was fascinated, not only by the attention arresting photograph, but by the ability to capture nature so easily! After that Raj just kept going back for more! He discovered the joys of waiting for the right moments to click as well as investing into a more powerful camera!

His thoughts verged into other things and soon the marking showed they were reaching the Cant. Paved roads, clean surroundings and well painted buildings signaled that that they were reaching their destination. Raj sighed as the vehicle raced finally through the Battalion location gates. He was hungry and was looking forward to the sumptuous spread usually served at the mess. He was not wrong. The cook had prepared a delicious menu of mutton curry and rice accompanied by a variety of vegetables. Shakti Singh, the cook, loved to pamper the bachelors and tried to create home menus for these "boys" who were away from their families!

More then that, the "izzat" or pride for the outfit was present in all the soldiers and cook Shakti Singh was no different! In fact cookhouse's had many anecdotes where the cooks invented amazing recipes out of nothing just to make sure the discipline of the 'table' was intact!

Talking about cookhouse capers pertaining to this feeling, one famous story did rounds about a "pretend cook!

The story goes that at an extreme post

one Captain found himself suddenly pulled into the social interaction net when a group of guests arrived at his remote post. This Army post had no cook. The Captain had been told to fend for himself for a week and then the cook would be send up. Luckily a soldier, in actuality the driver of the jeep, stepped forth and volunteered to cook for his "saab" till the arrival of the real cook. "I love to cook. When I go home it is me who makes all the meals!" said the "pretend" cook confidently. That day, before the guests arrived, since Captain saab was not averse to having butter "parathas"' till the ration supplies came in the evening, the cook had been quite relaxed. But now unexpected "ghchsts" (guests) were coming. That was serious. The "cook" with the never die attitude every soldier carries in the quest to ever let the "paltan" down went at the challenge full throttle.

Oh oh, however the 'pretend' cook discovered to his horror that even though Captain saab had ordered a good brunch for the unanticipated company, supplies only threw up methi vegetable. They were out of basics like onions, tomatoes, masalas! Red chilli being the only dry masala. Checking his pantry (a supply trunk) he saw a packet of instant noodles, lots of gram (chana) daal, bottle of tomato sauce, butter, "methi saag" and cashew nuts. Innovating as best as he could, he cooked a packet of instant noodles into the gram daal, to produce the famous "Noodle Walli daal"! Methi and cashews were kneaded into the dough to transform in to "Methi Parathas". Milk powder was shaped into the desert of "doodh ki tikki". The guests were suitably impressed when they were served tall glasses filled with a chilled exotic drink, (two tablespoon jam topped with cold water), right in the initial. To their mind seeing the extreme field conditions, they never predicted such culinary imagination evicting from the cookhouse! They were even more awed when brunch was served.

They ate, they drank and were conquered. Driving away they would have by no means visualized the `chaos' in the cook house when preparations for their meal had created. The pretend cook was given much praise, which he shyly accepted wondering what the fuss was about! But that was the army way of life, which is full of such anecdotes! They just had to make do with what was there and make it into something unforgettable!

As of now, Raj was not thinking of all that since he was busy tucking in the appetizing food and congratulating the cook for it!

•••

Next morning, at breakfast, Raj pierced the morsel of fish with a fork and ate it with some relish. Their battalion was on a hill-side and in a downward slant was a gushing river. Raj was actually sitting on a knob of the hill that directly jutted out into the river! A sun umbrella, a round table and some chairs completed the dining room! "Fresh fish, chips, eggs and juice", was on the menu. Shakti Singh, the cook, as said before, was always trying his hand at new recipes. Supplies were not always 'cordon bleu' and as we already know, sometimes very difficult to get since these were far-flung border areas. But that did not hamper the cook house at all. If tomatoes were not available for soup, large doses of tomato sauce spiced by 'masala' was used. If fresh veggies were late in arriving, onions, local roots and herbs graced the table. Fish was in abundance and that was a common item on the menu mostly!

Raj was not the only one enjoying this tasty repast in such delightful environs, his colleagues too sat eating breakfast with him.

" The tiger was magnificent! I regret not being able to capture the occurrence on camera." Raj interjected speaking of their experience the day before.

"Aha, yes your passion for photography is growing is it not? This is the place for you to add to your skills since the locations are unparalleled!" Commented Captain Prakash.

"Even the grass is vibrant, alive and crawling with wild life for potential shots!" Laughed someone.

"And then came the Leeches!"

Pulling off Leeches was a daily exercise here. Especially upscale hilly tracts. Leeches could be in the boots, clothes. Silently they stuck on to the skin and fattened up on the 'victims' blood-painlessly of course, before dropping off!

"I believe that the leeches here are longer than the normal leeches found elsewhere in the mountains and average 4-5 inches in length. They thrive up to an altitude of 12,000 ft above sea level." Parroted Captain Prakash as if he was directly reading it from a book!

"Hmmm! Yes I read that the Tiger leech one of the more famous varieties of leeches, which are found hereabouts!" Raj nodded

"I read that they can drink up to three times their body weight in blood and then hide for up to two months to digest." Laughed Prakash.

"I believe in some sciences leeches are used to suck impure blood...."

Their conversation shifted to more practical details for the day. A healthy discussion was underway soon.

Soon the Commanding officer, (CO), Colonel Alok Kher, who too was sitting with them for breakfast, discussed office with Raj. Just then, a polite cough made them aware of a messenger standing by waiting to be heard, "Sir this invitation has come for everyone," pronounced the messenger loudly.

Col Kher wiped his mouth with a napkin then turned his attention to the messenger.

"Hmmm? Now who is calling us?" Col Kher grunted taking the white invitation card. "Oh we all-yes all, have been invited to a 'soiree' at Mr Deb Sen's tea garden tomorrow!"

"Mr Sen? Is he not the one who apparently risked all his money and invested into a tea garden that has some bad history?" Raj curiously asked his CO.

"Poor fellow! I guess he shall never live that one down!"

"What is the story?' Captain Jones insisted on knowing.

"Many, many years ago, this particular location where his tea garden is was flooded due to an influx of rainwater brought on by severe flash floods! That was it! This garden was abandoned and thereafter lay unsold. Along came Mr Sen, who rubbished all claims that a flood could still strike and wash away his garden. He bought it some years ago and is quite happy!" Col Kher informed him.

"Very brave I must say!" Captain Jones nodded.

Suddenly Col Kher grinned, "Well, my breakfast binge is over, since I have to go home and tell my wife about the impending, aah, dinner invite! She needs time to plan for these swanky tea garden parties-as usual she will have nothing to wear!"

Everyone laughed at that. Mrs Lito Kher was adorable. She was quick witted and fun loving. As the commanding officer's wife she was the first lady of the battalion of some sorts. She actually guided the other ladies to adapt towards the social responsibilities expected from them towards the organization.

When Col Kher returned home, Lito, (actually Lalita), Kher sitting on the living room carpet, looked up from the tinsel, crepe paper and drawing sheets she was cutting. Next to her lay a big mug of coffee and one huge chocolate chip cookie grooming a fine china plate!

"Hello CO saab!" she merrily greeted her husband then quickly returned to what she was doing.

The living room was full of evidence that most of the 'object d arts' there, had been beautifully hand -made. Decoupage urns, water color handmade lamps and pin and thread wall paintings said it all. Of course it was all Lito's handiwork!

He stood watching her then his eyes travelled to the lone cookie.

"No you don't" Lito warned immediately catching his gaze yearningly staring at the biscuit.

"Awww, just half cookie?"

"Last evening you ate all of the one's I made at home. There is just one left and I intend to eat it!"

"Not fair old girl! You give a baking 'demo' on cookie making and not to forget conduct classes, ah on the same subject at a welfare meets; lucky ladies I must say! However it is not fair we never get a full fill of tasting!"

Lito grinned at her husband's banter. She decided to leave what she was doing.

"Awwwwwwwwww!" Lito stood up and stretched.

"I simply love my life!" she trilled! Snatching up the cookie and cup she walked out into the beautifully landscaped garden. Col Kher followed her.

The garden had been 'done up' by Lito. She had painted pots, stuck up bridges with thin bamboo sticks and made papier-mâché birds! Yes all by herself.

"I was telling the new bride, Divya, to stop being such a er...wim..! Lito just about stopped herself since the word she was going to use was hardly complimentary! Col Kher raised an eyebrow and grinned as she continued, "Aaah I was telling her, how much self- efficiency I have learnt in the army!" Lito picked up a papier-mâché bird. "All this-right from the papier-mâché bird to the Decoupage I learnt here. I so am looking forward to the classes Shivi (a unit lady) is giving on how to make plaster of Paris curios!"

"Oh, but I though this month's welfare meet is about learning rights and banking procedures-you invited an expert …?"

"Uh uh-curio class is for the next special meet... the ladies have requested it! As I was saying it is not only that, about curios and bakes, here I have learnt to be myself! The respect and learning is a different ball game altogether…!"

She stopped mid way since her husband now was openly laughing at her passion! He, in much amusement, offered by way of words,

"Yes on the new bride...I mean Divya, how is she doing?" Col Kher by now was sitting on a garden chair.

"Very badly –she is crying and missing home! We, as in the unit ladies, are taking her for a movie tomorrow evening, to cheer her up! Let her experience the open air theater charm and eat kebabs and vada's. She is stepping into a fresh, new adventurous kind of life-the army way of life! She has shuttered her outlook by just crying for the bright-lights of the city... uuuurgh, I wish her husband would tutor her on on these things, " Lito growled, "don't they get it? This life is glorious for us ladies. We live in an atmosphere of grace and "tereeka" (style)."

"Come, come, Lito she will learn!"

Then Col Kher frowned,

"Did you say tomorrow? Can't you take her for the movie tonight!" Col Kher said.

"Why?" Lito asked in surprise.

"We are all, the officers and their wives, are going for dinner to the Sen's tomorrow evening! He has been going on and on about how the army, rather our unit helped him when that elephant in his plantation was stuck in that muddy ditch......Sen is so grateful he is throwing a party to acknowledge our presence here! Moreover Sen is an army brat. His father served in the army so he is overjoyed to interact with us! As they say, fraternity bonds always are very strong!"

"Sen? Oh is he not the tea gardener who bought that garden which everyone said was a bad location?"

"Etu brutus? You too?"

"Am I wrong?" Lito persisted.

"Oh oh yes- yes, his tea garden is under a threat if ever there is a massive earthquake, landslide or floods since its location is really not good. But since nothing like that has happened for the last few years, Sen has taken a calculated risk! It is a small garden and he loves his choice, did you notice his garden is the only one within this vicinity the rest are some miles away!"

"Huh huh!" Lito nodded.

"Actually most feel he is stupid. But he says that there have been a few storms and one odd earth quake and nothing happened.."

"Then why such er doubt on his buy?"

"Well many years ago there *had been a disaster* in the form of floods and this garden suffered plenty. The then owners fled literally. For many subsequent years, till I guess two years ago, this place lay abandoned. *Then,* our Mr Sen decided to purchase it. He says why be negative? He thinks he is absolutely right." Repeated Col Kher once again as he had to his colleagues in the morning.

"Hmmm some would say that is the right attitude no? But suddenly why is everyone talking floods and disasters every where?"

"According to some studies the area above is just waiting to erupt with a natural calamities. So much of degradation, drilling and invasion by humans has weakened these areas. The MET department in its gloomy acknowledgement of global warming and pollution predicts freaky weather all the time...!"

"They-er could be right..?"

Col Kher shrugged and made his way back inside muttering something.

Lito ran after him, hardly catching most of what he said. She just exclaimed,

"Oh no! Such a short notice-I have nothing to wear...!"

Walking back in, Col Kher, guffawed! Lito looked miffed at his merriment. But her mind switched to the present quickly enough, 'hmm she could wear the black and red sari, combine it with.....!

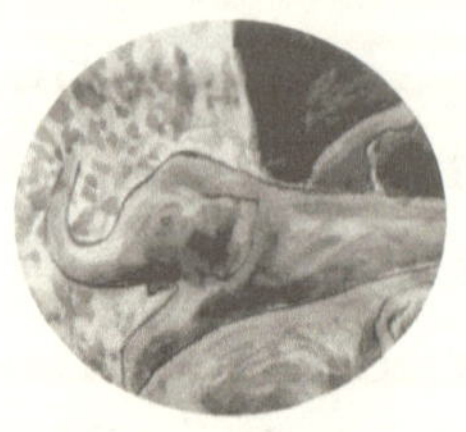

2

Lito Kher had come from a totally civilian background when she had married Col Alok Kher. At that time Lito was working with a key chain of hotels in housekeeping at New Delhi. It was a big decision to leave her job and get married to an Army man. Lito was so confused when she resigned and moved with her husband to a posting to Vishakhapatnam in the South of India. Visakhapatnam is a major sea port on the south east coast of <u>India</u>. It is the second largest city in the state of <u>Andhra Pradesh</u>. It has beautiful landscapes, beaches and hillocks,!

Lito loved the beauty of the place but had no idea how to fit into the confusing norms offered by an Army way of life.

"Lito please wait for the senior most "lady" to pick up a plate first at a buffet dinning meal!" Col Kher (then Major Kher), would advise her.

"Lito please try and dress appropriately when going for a welfare meet." He would add.

He would continually teach her on Mess regulations.

"What is a Mess?" Lito had actually innocently asked her new husband as they travelled by train for the first time to the Unit after marriage.

Controlling his amusement, Alok patiently explained, against the backdrop of the clatter of rails, "it is dining and living area that is used pertaining to very strict rules! The Indian Army too follows a system which is quite similar to the British. Presently a typical regiment/unit would have two messes: One for the commissioned officers, one for the Junior Commissioned Officers (JCO)." She nodded and settled further into her berth, very excited at that point to learn about her new life!

"The dining area for the troops is called the "Langar". In the 18th century the British Army called mess dining rules the Queen's regulations. A set of very formal rules were formatted for dining at the Mess during that time. A Mess consists of a formal Ante

Room or drawing room where the battalion trophies are displayed, a bar, a recreation room , a card room and most important the dining room." Said Alok . "Can you imagine earlier women were not invited into the ante room-it was solely a male domain. They were restricted to the ladies room. The only time they ate with the officers was during the Ladies Night! Dress code was/is very strict too. The Mess also has rooms to accommodate officers who needed them to stay in. Earlier, as mentioned, ladies were not permitted in the mess except if they were attending the ladies night dinners at the Mess. That had changed considerably now." Alok would inform Lito now and then. "But why were we not allowed?"

"Male bastion I guess!" Alok would tease her. But soon Lito realized following Mess regulations was a serious.

Lito soon learned that the Mess as far as the Indian Army organization is concerned is a very serious area of attention. May it be jungles, mountains or even plains your mess is an indication of your discipline!

"Lito please...you need to know.." Alok would begin his tutorage.

Wide- eyed, Lito would nod and try her best to follow all the social expectations her husband kept informing her of. However soon, as time passed, she was up to her teeth with all the instructions being given out.

Lito found her-self becoming sullen and angry. She would snap every time her husband advised her on something related to their social etiquette in regards to the army.

"Stop it! This way I shall not be able to think straight!" Lito snapped more than once at her husband. Alok would not know how to explain to her that this was it-living a life in the army required certain disciplines!

Then one day it all changed.

There was a huge dinner to welcome in the new Commanding Officer and his wife to the battalion. The party was thrown at the battalion Mess.

Lito was a little balked when she entered the party. All the officers were dressed in impressive uniforms, specially meant for these occasions. Women glittered in graceful saris. The room was enchantingly bespoke of the 'ye olde 'charm of the yester years.

Trophies, paintings and memorabilia, a heady reminder of the Battalion's successes in many operations involving the defense of the country, adorned the space! A different type of atmosphere prevailed. An atmosphere where politeness and a way of doing things socially correct prevailed!

Lito, unsure and a little overwhelmed by the whole grandeur of her surroundings stood aside surveying the groups of people around.

"What a lovely place this is! Oh I am dying to visit the beaches and the temples!" A husky voice said. Lito turned to espy a tall lady dressed in a pink sari, her hair tied in a chignon with a pink rose tucked into the side of her bun. Lito stared in fascination at the obvious picture of grace and beauty. Everything the lady did from holding her soft drink or even patting her hair was a picture of style. A small group of ladies surrounded her. Suddenly the previous Commanding officer's wife noticed Lito and she extended a hand and called her. "Lito meet our new commanding officer's wife Mrs Kamana Malhotra." The lady who had arrested Lito's attention so vividly, gave a slight stately nod. "Kamana, this is a new entrant into the battalion, Lalita Kher-better known as Lito!"

Lito awkwardly moved forward to join the group.

"Well, Well, Well, now here is a pretty bride!" Kamana warmly interjected.

Lito blushed and swallowed in unsure confusion.

"Lito? May I call you Lito?"

"Y-Yes...please." Lito nodded.

"Aha so how is the army treating you? Um I guess the social do 's and do not's get to you right?" She gave a mock click of her thumb and finger and pointed at Lito in askance.

Lito flushed.

"Hmmm I have seen that look before..."

Mrs Malhotra smiled in understanding; but did not take up on the issue there and then, and embarrass the badly self conscious Lito. However, in the subsequent days she took special care of Lito. She made sure Lito understood the gravity of discipline required by the armed forces set up even when not on duty. "Charity begins at home!" Was her favourite comment.

Lito soon learned how gracious it was to follow the correct norms and keep strict discipline. She felt herself somehow growing in confidence. Her appreciation of this unique way of life began to take shape. She looked forward to the adventurous verticals presented when you visited a new place.

Her life was full and bustling. Her mind never bored. She loved welfare meets, theme ladies meets and alongside all the seminars and lectures emitting from this. She was given responsibilities, which had multi-pronged effect of making her confident and even a public speaker. The first time Lito had to go on stage was frightening however!

"I am simply going to die-why do I need to go on stage and blabber about gardening techniques?" She hissed at her husband one evening prior to the event.

"You know our soldier's wives come from remote areas and they do not have the exposure to many things we take for granted. It is your duty to share things with them!" Alok intoned almost primly. Lito knew all of that but just could not quell the butterflies.

The welfare meet ensured at a large gathering. Lito felt the butterflies tango in the pit of her stomach. She was so nervous that she had to actually control her shaking body by clenching her fists and teeth.

As we know, Lito had to go on stage to talk about the new gardening techniques. She had researched very well. The walk towards the stage was one fraught with tension and misgivings. Lito was sure she would make a fool of herself! When she was on stage she croaked, "good m-morning…!" the mike squealed and squawked. Lito thought she would faint. A silence ensued. She looked at the sea of expectant faces. To her mind they were serious, formal faces! She was so stressed by now that she was thinking of running off the stage and hiding where no one could find her.

Then she looked at Kamana sitting right in the front row. Kamana serenely looked at Lito. Then in all formal atmosphere of great seriousness, Kamana, making sure no one was looking, made a comical face by rolling her eyes, sticking out her tongue and then she gave a big wink and a thumbs up gesture. Her stylish way of doing things just did not match up to her antics! But this had a dramatic effect on Lito! A giggle escaped Lito-it turned into a wide smile. The crowd watching her relaxed at the giggle and clapped. Suddenly they seemed friendly and encouraging faces. That acted like a confidence boosting measure! Smiling she just started to talk! After that she was able to begin her lecture! Lito just loved the entire episode! "Aha Lito you did well!" Kamana said later. "Don't mind my facial encouragements-but darling I had to push you out of the apparent stage fright you portrayed so brilliantly there!"

Lito stammered a shy "thanks".

Lito became an eager learner. Mrs Malhotra became her inspiration. "The lady is a thorough ..well...*a lady!* She never talks out of turn, she makes excuses for the other's failings and she is always there! I am going to be like her when you are senior officer!" Lito would breathlessly say to her husband off and on.

•••

AT THE SEN'S PARTY.....

"The tea plant needs a hot, moist climate. It grows in temperatures ranging from 10 -30 degrees Centigrade, in areas with an average yearly rainfall of 2,000 mm. and at a ground level of between 600-2000 meters above sea level..." Deb Sen was explaining earnestly to a assembly of guests at his party.

A low hum of party chatter and audible conversations floated in the background; joined by the levels of other sounds. Waiters swished in silent efficiency between the guests.

The Sen's had a beautiful house that merged with the ethnicity of the place.

Raj sipped his drink and did a once all over. Fairy lights twinkled and adorned the garden bushes surrounding the lawns. Light music permeated the air.

The warmth of the welcome they got was not lost him. He noticed Prakash standing in a corner with the group talking to Deb. A pity his wife refused to come, so Prakash was here alone. Divya seemed to be giving poor Prakash a tough time.

Tea planters here in these areas were quite closely associated with the army units being posted in. Since the battalion had arrived they had visited quite a few tea plantations on invites. In turn they too had invited the planters to the mess.

Raj was very fascinated by the fact that the tea planters actually lived in a time wrap. Every plantation had its ways and styles. They still had the rules of etiquettes followed during the Raj. They had huge houses with umpteen domestic helpers. High tea, gala's flower shows and baking expertise was a way of life here. Clubs assured the men played games with discipline. Something like the army! Life could get very lonely otherwise since plantations were huge and far apart. But there seemed to be bond between them! Most remained in one place for years and adapted their lives completely to these environs. So many stories of encounters with wild life, old village tales and some style of functioning was respected very much. Raj recalled what he read about the discovery of tea! It was believed as a colonial myth that the Assam tea bush was discovered by one <u>Robert Bruce</u>, a <u>Scottish</u> adventurer, who apparently noticed locals making tea from the leaves of a wild bush. It is said that it was not until the early 1830s that Robert's brother, Charles, had the leaves examined at the botanical gardens in Kolkata.

Just then Shaila Sen rushed up and in a complete gush, bordering on a tinge of hysteria asked "Major Raj, I hope you are being looked after? Did you try the baby corn quiche? Try..."

Raj said, "Thank you Ma-am." Short polite conversation ensued.

"Our garden is very small, and sales limited, but we love it here. I know people think we have been stupid investing in this location...anyhow have you seen the other gardens? They are huge, with worker quarters, clubs everything; *even wild visitors!* I believe the tea garden in the north actually had visits from tigers who growl in a sing song way??!" Shaila began to regale him with stories about myths and tales so typical of these places.

Shaila's eyes caught another group and she excused herself smiling charmingly , this way she flitted from one group to the other in this vein; proving to be a warm, caring hostess.

Raj's attention was suddenly diverted by the tinkle of trinkets. He turned and noticed a little girl staring at him. She was wearing a bright pink party frock. Her hair was in two neat plaits. Her wrists were adorned by silver bangles that tinkled as she moved. Her oval face had a sweetness to it, her eyes were alert and bright.

"Hello?" Raj in askance said.

"Hello! I am Tinku Sen!"

"Hello Tinku I am Major Raj."

She flicked a braid and without any introduction to what followed she started as if mid sentence, ".....and I told Dumpu that he is very naughty and he should not eat sugar...but he never listens to me!"

Raj smiled and continued to listen to her prattle. "Do you want to meet Dumpu-oh Dumpu would love to meet an Army Officer.. come come!"

Raj assuming Dumpu was her sibling just followed her. Expertly Tinku led him through the house. The sound of their footfalls clattering loudly on the wooden floor. She led into the back garden and further into the columns of tea bushes. Raj was now more then curious. Suddenly Tinku stopped.

Raj started. A huge shadowy outline swayed against the evening light in their way. *Dumpu was an elephant!*

Tinku held out her palm. Dumpu, seemingly a very young elephant stretched his trunk and nuzzled her palm. He was quite distinct. In the focus lights hauled up on trees for the party, Raj could clearly see that Dumpu had a festive bell tied around his neck. His fore feet were adorned with bright multi-coloured anklets that tinkled! "Tinkle-dim dim-- tinkle tinkle-dim dim". His little tusks, jutting out from the sides of his mouth, were painted too! Dumpu shook and swayed in greeting.

A little stumped, Raj stood very still. Elephants could be quite unpredictable with strangers. "Come Dumpu wants to shake hands!" Tinku urged the Major. Tentatively Raj extended a palm. Dumpu nuzzled his palm with his trunk too. Raj grinned. Dumpu seemed to like him!

"Oi Tinku baba-you in the gardens so late?" A gruff voice suddenly interrupted.

"Dasuda meet Raj....Dumpu likes him!"

"*Namaste Saab*! I am Dumpu's Mahout!" An elderly man dressed in a dhoti and sleeveless vest came forward.

"*A pet elephant here?*" Raj asked in surprise after returning the greetings.

Dasuda came and stood next to Raj and in low voice explained, "Dumpu's mother was captured by poachers. Dumpu however managed to run away. Abandoned, he witlessly ran into the gardens. He was just a baby. We rescued him and I came to live here to take care of Dumpu. He roams freely in the gardens and is every ones friend! We tried to release him into the jungles but after a walk or even night out he always is back here to this very spot!"

Dumpu indeed had escaped sure capture when he was very young. No one would believe it, but Dumpu still had fresh memories about that terrible day. It made him scared and insecure. He still missed his mother.

Dumpu story of losing his mother began one bright sunny day. That day seemed like one of the most promising days ever in Dumpu's young eyes. The sun shone, a

cool light breeze rustled up a rasp through the foliage that sounded like natures music provided just for Dumpu's pleased mood! So it seemed then! The water in the ponds sparkled with emerald green polish, inviting the will to splosh and splash! There was a certain contentment in the air that made Dumpu very happy and jaunty. He was forever scuttling here and there trying to channelize his high spirited restlessness. The herd had moved into the pond. The cool waters did more to raise the contentment barometer immediately. His mother was teasingly showering him by sucking up water from the pond and spraying it all over him. Dumpu hit the waters with his head and tried to suckle some to shower too!

Soon they walked out of the pond. Dumpu the baby of the herd had a protective ring of herd members around him. Close on his heels was his mother. *She did not let him out of her sight at all!* They were trying to find a sunny spot when it happened. Unexpectedly Dumpu with playful naughty intent ran away from the herd and his mother towards the other side. Leaving the herd his mother ran after him. Mindless exhilaration encouraged Dumpu to run as fast as his small legs could take him. He plunged into thickets and wild hedges loving the entire excitement it caused. His mother trumpeted a warning and chased after him. Dumpu was not listening! He just ran. They came up into a clearing and without warning his mother fell into a well camouflaged pit, *set by poachers!* She gave out a loud trumpet as she stumbled and fell. Frightened at her tone, Dumpu turned ran back. He tried to find her. When he saw where she was, he helplessly ran around the huge, deep pit crying for her to come to him. The herd was up ahead and were walking opposite the wind so could not pick up any sounds or smells really. They most likely heard nothing since no sounds carried. Dumpu in total panic tried to jump into the pit too, when suddenly half a dozen men brandishing guns clanging vessels, and yelling at the top of their voices surrounded the pit. Dumpu was so alarmed that he fled. He ran for hours, little realizing he was running away from the jungle and towards human habitation. It is here he stumbled into the tea garden where Dasuda found him. He never left the vicinity. He loved little Tinku and welcomed the calm life the tea garden provided. By trial and error he became quite domesticated!

Presently Tinku took over conversation with her nonstop chatter. She pulled out some sugar lumps and giggled as Dumpu hungrily gobbled them up. Raj too was given the honour by her to feed Dumpu!

Later at dinner, Raj was still quite taken by this experience of meeting an elephant so up close and personal!

He related the whole incident on the way back. They all had come for the party together like a big family, distributed in three vehicles. Raj was with the Colonel and Lito, as well as Prakash. They were totally fascinated by his account! Prakash also told them a tale of a group of elephants who played a prank with a returning group of party goers. "We all know here group of wild elephants have to be given a wide berth! These folks in their jeep stopped on seeing a herd crossing. They were very quiet. The elephants crossed and all heaved a sigh! They waited a while to make sure that the elephants had gone."

"Then?" Lito gasped

"The elephants sneaked around to the back of the vehicle and startled the living daylights out of them by abruptly trumpeting!"

"Omigosh did they attack...?"

"Ha ha ha ha no the driver drove like ghosts were chasing him...ha ha! He went aaaaaahhhhhh vroooooooooooom! He just vanished so fast...ha ha ha"

They all burst into helpless laughter.

•••

Divya stared at the wall. She had churlishly refused to attend the Sen party. Now boredom had eaten into her insides. She hit a fist in her palm and swore, "Damn this place....no one seems to notice what a back of beyond area this is. OOOOH! That day all the ladies twittering and chattering at the picnic...grrrr it makes me so mad to think they have no ideas of the latest trends, the latest anything. Why are they so thrilled with nature I wonder??"

Over the weekend the unit had driven to a beautiful spot for a picnic. Games had been organized too. It was great fun except Divya did not think so. She looked appalled that everyone was cycling around and playing cricket. The ladies too! They did not mind the sun or open air intrusions into their clothes and skin. Divya sat under a portable umbrella the whole time and refused to join the fun and games. Now, in her drawing room, she gritted her teeth and brooded over her bad luck for coming to this location. Her anger increased when she heard her husband return from the party in high happy spirits. She did not greet him when he entered instead she rose from the armchair and returned inside to the bedroom. Prakash shrugged and headed to the kitchen for a glass of water. This had been the prevailing atmosphere in the house ever since Divya had come here. Prakash wondered what would change his wife's idea about the army way of life?

The Cant area was beautiful. Enclave housing dotted landscapes. The mess was placed in the hilly cover of groves. Today, Lito had invited the unit ladies over for a garden lunch over to her house called 'the Tiger Villa'. The officers had all left for a conference to another military station. The ladies would spend time together.

Umbrella's and round tables spread across her garden. Lito wearing an attractive blouse over blue jeans played perfect host.

The ladies were treated to a mix of French and Mexican cuisine planned and cooked by Lito herself! "You know the electricity went off and the blender stopped. I almost thought we would have to shelf pate' (pate de foie gras) and crackers! But the electricity popped back and here we have the famous mock pate made with chicken instead of goose liver!"

"Yum, I am glad the lights came on-fancy you inventing your own method of pate!"

Said Savitri Yadhav giggling and munching the cracker. Savitri's husband was the second in command or 2IC of the battalion.

"Gosh, I am so glad, Mrs Rehli gave this super idea and recipe for mock Pate ! Otherwise tracking goose liver would have meant something!"

Divya stood aside, her face frozen, not reacting to any conversations.

Lito and two other ladies, Bela and Priya, walked up to her. Divya managed a wintry acknowledgment.

"Hi Divya, how are you?"

"Fine." Divya fidgeted and looked uncomfortable.

"Has your house been done up?"

"I-er I...." Somehow their words welled up self pity and no words came forth instead there were tears. To every ones shock Divya began to cry.

Lito immediately put her arms around her and led her inside.

"Divya what is the matter? Is there a problem with your husband?"

"Oh no-no, Mrs Kher (sniff) it is not him---" Divya sniffed sitting down on an armchair.

"Wooof woof woof!"

An enormous golden retriever, the Kher's pet, came bouncing to her. He was called Snuggy Woo!,

Now Snuggy Woo was the comic relief and much pampered pet of the Kher household. Ever since Ishan and Angat, the Khers two sons had moved to hostel in the hills of Himachal Pradesh, Snuggy Woo became the complete center of attention and hopeless spoiling in this home! He felt so special; trotting around with this extra edge in his street!

Not used to his very huge affectionate greetings thwarted, he bounced around in silly glee to as if saying to Divya "hey stop reacting it is *me* Snuggy Woo the incredible dog!"

"Aiiieeeeeeeee oh please....dog......I am scared!" Divya dramatically cried.

"Down Snuggy - Wo ... NOOO!" Lito yelled.

What followed is the usual chaos that transpires when anyone tries to instantly discipline a pet who feels he is above all! Snuggy with brown dripping eyes stood on both his hind legs whacking Lito's grabbing hands his fat front paws. That had Lito helplessly in giggles but seeing Divya;s cold remote unimpressed expression, Lito desperately tried to hold Snuggy. Oh oh Snuggy found a new lap. Divya's. Ignoring the fact he carried so many extra pounds he jumped and tried to sit once again on his reluctant target.

Divya was hysterical. She pushed, screamed and almost kicked Snuggy off. In all this Snuggy actually stopped and in confusion stared at her. Lito managed to calm her and pull at the resisting Snuggy who thought a game had ensued. He scampered, wagged and bounced much to Divya very voluble dismay.

Catching hold of a newspaper Lito folded it and rustled it. Snuggy was so petrified of the sound that it worked wonders always to quell an antic attack by him, if ever. The newspaper threat was rarely used. But today the dreaded discipliner was brought out. Tail between legs Snuggy settled into a corner, looking sad and reproachful.

Lito hated doing that but she turned to the sullen guest and mentally agreed there was no other way.

Snuggy Wo looked stricken at this rejection. But due to Lito's persistence of dragging him away, the newspaper rustle, soon things settled.

Divya sat with hands crossed over her chest.

With a low sniffle, intruding her slightly defiant tones, Divya said, "it is this place. It is so dead. So boring...back home in Mumbai I have a life. I have no life here."

"But you are with your husband who..."

"Here my husband has routine!" Divya interrupted a trifle rudely, but Lito maturely kept her calm.

"5.30 PT then work and office, home for lunch, *then* 4.30 games, *then* back home, *then* he wants to sit in the garden to watch birds or take treks to spot wild life! We are together all the time! But nowhere to go! We have no shopping malls...oh...oh!" Divya almost bawled.

"Divya any new bride would die for a life like that! Would you rather he was a businessman or a corporate guy who leaves the house and returns only late evening. His work being entirely his own and you as a wife play no role in his organization. It is so different here-try and open your eyes.... An Army man is so happy to be within his home and hearth since he values its comfort so…. !"

Divya's face crumbled and she began to sob into the tissues Lito had sympathetically provided.

Lito let her cry then patted her and abruptly, "You are married now." she paused then said, "he values the comfort of home and hearth because his job is not ordinary." "What do you mean?" Divya looked up to ask. "Our men defend the country. It is not an ordinary task. You should be so respectful and proud to know that!" Lito held.

"Oh I know all that but…!" Divya shrugged not really giving Lito the satisfaction of knowing that if her point had got across. However Lito continued,

"That is one point. Second point is we have a way of life here. If you stop being so absorbed you will realize you are so fortunate to be who you are-an Army man's wife. Malls, shops all can be done but who gets to sit in a garden with grass that is so alive with creatures or take a boat across these rivers or just have the presence of being a lady wife who is so respected! You know there a common parley that says 'in my next birth god make me an Army man's wife! You know why?"

"No?" Divya uncrossed her arms and indifferently twirled the corner of her hair and stared ahead. Lito shrugged but continued to explain anyhow,

"We are different! We learn to beat all odds and make our lives wonderfully rich. We see places, we bond, and we never judge. No cast, no creed just us like a family you will realize and love the ethos..you know. I was present when Savitri had her little girl. No family member of hers could make it- so we filled in since we were her family now--- so on so forth."

Lito paused. Divya like any young girl did not pay attention. She was restless and apathetic.

"Ok." Lito said firmly. "You are new and not very familiar with life in a military station. Actually I did not disturb you since I thought you needed time to adjust. But I guess I would love your company!"

"H-how?"

"Tomorrow as a welfare project, along with two ladies, I am planning to go to our

"Jawans" homes and interact with their wives. I shall pick you up at eleven."

Divya not too excited, nodded.

"Now let us be social-I mean let us join the others in the garden! Hmmmm-let us put on a big smile and have fun!"

Snuggy who had been relegated to a corner with strict orders not to move, hearing her change of tone sprang up and happily shook his tail. Lito's stern "NO," and a rustle from the paper, pushed him right back. He settled back with a grumpy groan. It smote Lito's heart to do that but Divya looked as if she would again have a hysterical attack if Snuggy so much as wagged a tail in her direction!

"Clap, clap, clap!" Ladies I have planned games." Lito announced walking into the garden with Divya.

For the next two hours, Divya included, had the time of their lives. Lito had started up a truth and dare game, which graduated into a hilarious event!

The men folk unexpectedly returned and all of them barged into the garden lunch. Much hilarity followed as they too had to play truth and dare. Later a sumptuous lunch was served.

"The soufflé is delicious Ma'am!" Raj complimented Lito.

"Thanks Raj-I am glad that proper food is here today. Day before when you bachelors did a gate-crash at midnight demanding food I had to cook 'Aloo' Parathas   oooo! Who cooks that in the middle of the night??" Her wide smile took the sting out of her words.

"Ma am-but we loved them –best is we gate crashed Major Chandra's house last to last week and Mrs Chandra actually had to rustle up daal -chawal after midnight-she was as sporting as you....!"

Bachelors gate-crashing demanding food was very much a part of the armed forces tradition. All married officers were up for the gate crash threat. But no one minded!

"Have you raided Divya and Prakash yet?"

"No ma-am! But let you into a secret we are doing that tonight! We plan to have "aandha (eggs) bhujiya and paratha demand menu!"

"Gasp-you devils!"

"She is a new bride and we need to welcome her!"

"Absolutely! Sigh! I wish we could come along too!"

"Ma-am why not? It will be fun and incase her cooking skills are not up to the mark, you ladies can chip in and um feed us!"

"Ahaa! Yes and so you, very *privileged*, bachelors get to eat anyways!"

"Ma-am it will be fun!"

"HMMMM! Let me ask the others and Col Kher!"

5

Raj rang the door bell. Everyone was absolutely quiet. There was no response in the quietness usually spreading in the dead of the night. Their shadowy group intent on raiding Divya and Prakash's home for food hardly noticed the background nocturnal sounds or even the fact that it was a moonless night. Sneaking into the complex with utmost excitement the Bachelor group had increased to include four couples too!

"Ting ting ting" Once again Raj pressed the bell.

"Someone is coming!" Lito giggled.

"Sssssh" Savitri warned.

"Och a snail is tickling my left leg!"

Fatima stamped her foot.

"shoo shooo haat!" a hissing whisper from the back of group as Lt Mehta chased away a curious stray dog!

"Ooey A leech stuck itself on my arm!"

murmured another pulling off the leech with a grimace.

"SSSHHHH!"

"Here he comes!" Raj whispered as a shadow reflected over the glass portion of the door.

A very drowsy Captain Prakash opened the door.

"SURPRISE!"

Col Kher, the Unit Officers and their wives hollered.

"Awwww-um g-good e-evening Sir !" Prakash dumbly mumbled soon getting his wits. They all stood, past midnight on his door-step!

Soon,

"Welcome, welcome thanks for targeting me as the gate-crashed victim!" He grinned good naturedly and let them in.

The ladies sang "Divya, Divya, *Divya!*"

There was no appearance.

Prakash's face shadowed but forcing a smile he went inside the bedroom mumbling over his shoulder, "just wake her up ...will be back in a second...".

Everyone waited.

"Are you out of your mind-its past midnight-

are they heathens or what? No way am I making food….!" Divya almost screeched.

"Ssssssssh-keep your voice down. Divya please, *please* don't do this-it is a tradition-do this for me!"

"Get out!"

"Shhhhh!"

"Get out! I am not coming to meet these uuuughnn!" Divya shifted and turned on her bed.

Prakash shrugged and returned to the living room.

"She is just um join…!" He stopped short. The room was empty

No one was there! They had all left.

Prakash was livid. He turned around and angrily stormed back into the room. Divya was startled at his fury. She sat up in bed and almost cringed. Prakash spat, "see they have left…groan this is so embarrassing… why Divya why??? How can you behave so rudely…what is your problem?"

Divya with a slow look of defiance spreading over her features hurled back, "I hate this life…I cannot be here….it is like they all gang up and have this family so er c- cohesive….whatever…. that sets me out.

I feel so left out."

"Because you refuse to be a part of anything!" Prakash fumed leaving the room.

Divya curled up in bed and began to cry. She missed home so badly that it hurt. Divya came from Chennai. She had a busy life in the bustling city. Her parents owned a luxurious apartment in a high rise complex. He father was a corporate person. He was working for a large multi-national company. Divya's mother worked at a bank. Divya was their only child. She was quite used to 'alone time'. Her parents were always out and she had to pretty much manage things on her own; notwithstanding the fact that she loved this city life. By twenty years of age, she was expertly driving her own car and merrily, independently whizzing around the city, doing exactly as she pleased. She never took up a job. Her parents were rich and gave in to all her material demands at the drop of a hat. Beauty salons, endless shopping sprees with her friends, as well as eating at the best restaurants filled her life! Divya loved wearing high heeled shoes. Her collection of expensive shoes ranged to almost twenty! This was the only life she knew. Interacting with neighbours at their swanky high rise apartment was restricted to polite interchanges only. Since her parents remained at work most part of the day and Divya at school, then college, Divya never really saw the comfortable bonhomie with people she was witnessing now.

She met Prakash at a party. It was love at first sight. Divya found Prakash incredibly solid and reliable! She loved his endearing courtesies towards women and his correct social etiquettes. After a whirlwind courtship they were married. Till then the whole idea of marrying an army officer was filled with romantic notions of the brave job he was doing protecting the borders. When Divya joined Prakash here she was horrified at what was expected from her. She had no love for the picturesque flat they were staying in. To her electricity going, water coming on timings at this far flung border area was something out of a horror fiction. She blinded herself to the facts that Cant's were so efficient in these inclement areas. She never saw the need to live up these moments that translated into stirring adventures and not waste time complaining. She yearned for instant material gratification. This place provided none and Divya burned with disgust at this! She hated the nature walks her husband so loved. "Mosquitoes, wind and dirty tracks mess up my skin and hair!" she would wail. Once whilst trying to get into a gypsy vehicle she broke a well painted nail. She cried for almost two hours and it took Prakash quite a long time to pacify her! "Why can't I wear a short dress for a "Bara Khana" (meal with the troops). To be controlled in her wardrobe was another heavy price Divya felt she was paying. "Darling dress with grace.... you have to follow certain disciplines...I cannot explain it er but wearing a plunging décolleté, black mini dress for this function is just not appropriate..." Prakash would helplessly try to explain. Then came the point when she had to wear sturdy footwear since the gradients did not allow stilettos! "Good for you Divs at least you want torture your back with those enormous stilts you wear!" Prakash joked as they hunted for suitable shoes for Divya. Divya was furious. Her mind clouded and blocked any friendly endeavours made by everyone. She became withdrawn and cold. She refused to see the adventure in her new life style. "Divs this is temporary-we do get posted to cities also... so enjoy this place and look forward to the other??!" Prakash tried to say but Divya refused to listen. She lost herself into her grumpy space. But today she realized she had gone too far. Guilt tore her insides. But she refused to acknowledge it. Tossing and turning she tried to sleep-managing to take her thoughts away from this event she began to think about the latest collection of shoes her friend had told her about over the phone. When Prakash, who had thundered off for a walk returned, Divya was fast asleep.

"Honestly this is the limit!" Savitri grumbled as the entire group walked back home. They all stayed in close vicinity.

"How can she shout and talk like that?" Priya frowned.

The entire assembly in the living room had heard Divya's outburst. They had politely left, as not to further embarrass poor Captain Prakash.

"You know what I think I am going to forgive her!" Lito announced when the group walked back to their respective homes.

"Grand of you ol girl!" Col Kher patted her proudly.

Lito peering into the shadowy faces confirmed why, "she really has no idea of bonding, ethos and all that-she is just a month old! We need to understand that!" Deep down somewhere Lito remembered how her first CO's wife Kamana Malhotra had handled her when *she* was getting used to this very new way of life. Today Lito wanted to emulate the same patience and understanding herself.

"I agree." Her husband nodded.

"We all can gang up and ostracize her but we as mature adults will be failing ourselves!"

There was a silence at these profound words.

Lito giggled, "see the humour....ha ha ha!"

They all burst out laughing trudged back home with the threads of humour stitching in their further conversations!

Tinku allowed her mother to braid her hair. Wearing shorts and a tee shirt, Tinku finally satisfied that she was dressed, ran out into the gardens. It was eleven AM and the tea workers all out in the garden. The sun was bight and air crisp. Tinku skipped along the rows of tea bushes throwing greetings hither thither before she finally reached the shed, skirting around it she arrived at the outer garden space by which you walked through towards the surrounding jungles.

Dumpu immediately trumpeted a greeting. Tinku ran up and fed him sugar lumps. "Tinku so early up again...!"

"Dasuda I am the luckiest girl in the world. I do home schooling. Today Ma is busy so I get an unscheduled off! In real schools the summer vacations are on Dasuda so I can get some days off too!"

Tinku was home schooled. This was a system followed by many over there due to the lack of proper schools or even the distances to good school. Some parents of planters taught their children at home then had them give certified exams when the time came. Shaila Sen decided to home school Tinku till her middle school. Tinku was a bright student and was learning her lessons as good as anyone of her age in other cities where schools were!

"Dasuda please take me with you on a jaunt with Dumpu."

The elderly Mahout grinned. After fifteen minutes Tinku astride Dumpu swayed out of the gardens.

Once they had exited the gardens the landscapes yielded to a sloppy pitch. "Giggle!" Tinku would hold her tickling tummy as Dumpu went down then up in sync with the inclines. They reached an area by the riverside and Dumpu was quite content to walk alongside the narrow water body. Dasuda stopped to pick up some herbs from the abundance of trees around and Tinku too slipped off Dumpu. She led Dumpu to the edge of the waters that had a natural dried mud beach like shore! Tinku threw off her slippers and dipped her toes into the water. Dumpu was not the one to be left behind either. Very gingerly he immersed his big front feet into the waters too! Tinku stroked his leg that was parked right next to her and softly she began to sing an ancient folk song Dasuda had taught her.

"I need some supplies so we are just going to the village." Dasuda interrupted this reverie.

"Come Dumpu now we ride to the village!" Tinku sprang up; hurriedly wore her slippers and mounted Dumpu.

The village was not much of a distance. It was a very small village. Urchins greeted Dumpu's presence with loud hoots and cheers. Ignoring them Dumpu halted near a tree to allow Tinku to slip off, which she did with practiced expertise.

Dasuda walked off to the row of shops lining one side. Tinku skipped towards the village square that was a huge banyan tree with a cemented platform surrounding it. Tinku saw a strange looking man sitting cross-legged addressing a motley of curious villagers. His out-fit was long flowing robes accentuated by a dark beard and kohl rimmed eyes. She moved nearer and she could hear the strangely dressed man say, "I do not predict any mumbo jumbo---it is common sense...for years we have had no angry weather but I was up there in the mountains...I could sense the brewing storms....no one is safe...no animal or human if a flood ensues.....THE FLOODS ARE COMING BE WARNED WE ALL SHALL DIE....TAKE PRECAUTIONS...!"

Tinku went all wide eyed. "TinKu let us go!" Dasuda urged/

"Dasuda who is he?" Tinu pointed to the strange man.

"Oh that is Binka...he actually was working with the weather department at one time but left his job to become a wanderer... oddly he now predicts weather conditions and all! Till now all his predictions have been wrong...but..."

"Dasuda he says we will all die...floods are coming!"

"Tinku don't listen to all this, come we have to return."

Tinku, once astride Dumpu bent forward and hugged her pet, "Dumpu I will never let you down...come what may I shall save you from floods....!" Her little heart beat faster as she imagined Dumpu running helter/skelter in case floods hit their areas. "Dasuda you yourself told me other wild animals instinctively run away to safety during natural calamities! They just vanish- you said that remember?" "Hmmm." Dasu nodded. "But Dumpu is just a pet....he will not..." Tinku whispered in a scared voice.

"Arre Tinku baby, hush nothing will happen....Dumpu will run away *from harms way!*"

"But Dasuda...."

Their voices faded as they crossed the gates leading into the Sen gardens.

•••

The day they were doing visits to the soldiers residence to meet up with their families, Lito negotiated her car into Divya's driveway and hooted. Savitri, Priya and Fatima were in the car too so it was a squeeze.

Lito had a small car, which she called her "Jalopy."It was bright red and managed to lift her mood greatly always. Driving herself gave her an independence, which she treasured.

"Mrs Kher, remember when we learned driving in Vishakapatnam?" Savitri giggled.

"And Fatima had her head out of the car window shouting "dekho dekho", when I was on the wheel!"

"Yes..the instructor almost went crazy. Four hysterical ladies reacting to every stone, cycle ,car on the road!"

This memory dissolved them into such humour that they giggled helplessly.

But the same mood was not prevailing with Divya.

Divya rushed out and sat in the backseat seat with a huff. "Hello there too!" Lito grinned, backing the car to return to the road. Savitri turned around from the front seat to say hello. Priya and Fatima grinned too. Divya just barely nodded. No mention of the fiasco last evening came.

"Thanks Divya for coming to this welfare with us, it is very important to interact with our soldiers families since these ladies come from all over the country like us. But the only thing is most come from deep interiors and suddenly displaced into this very different world can be a little confusing. But they love to rise to any occasion expected of them...." Lito chatted to fill the vacuum Divya's presence brought in the car. The other ladies were quite miffed otherwise of her behavior the night before.

Climbing a steep hill they reached the first house. The hostess, one of the soldier wives, they intended to visit, ran out in welcome. She was from Bengal. Dressed in a Bengali style of sari she was so pretty. Her house was spic and span. Lito and the ladies sat and chatted with her. In the course of their conversation they told her about how important it was to vaccinate children, be hygienic and remain fit. The day played out very well. Divya tried not to remain involved and seem sulky but the warmth of these meeting got to her. She could imagine how simple these folks were. How pure and loving. But unfortunately Divya discovered a leech stuck on her ankle. "ooooey....yech ......aaaah!" she raised unnecessary hell. Even though Lito and the others pulled it off and assured her nothing amiss was going to affect her health, she became quiet and glum. She also got time to stupidly put her mind back to her list of complaints. Seething inwardly Divya managed to convince herself that in some twisted ways these ladies were ganging up against her and actually influencing her husband to think badly of her. Their goody attitude made her look so bad! This added to her grievances even more. Later when they were returning and planning to stop at Savitri's house for refreshments, she again maintained her sulk. She was quiet and cold. She refused to enter Savitri's house and decided to walk home from there. Lito shrugged off the leading looks her companions gave her. "Let her be I am sure she will come around!" Lito whispered out of earshot range to Savitri who sharply glanced at her with disbelief.

7

Some days later, one evening, Divya still brooding, tried to wear a sari. She was still miffed with Prakash after the huge fight they had earlier. However she was a little apprehensive since deep down she knew her behavior was becoming unforgivable; especially with the unit ladies still so friendly and welcoming. Today as a small gesture she agreed to go for the "Bara Khanna" with the others.

At this event the officers and the troops would meet for a social evening hosted by the troops themselves. The food was prepared at the "Langar".

Langar is the place where soldiers have their meals. Here filling food is expected to satisfy robust appetites of hard working troops, and is the only predictable Mantra followed here. The bill of fare is decided for the week and followed unfailingly. But somewhere the regional influences seep in. Like even if the menu says Daal Chawal, it is not surprising to see in a Maharastrain troops Langar, a tray full of ground, fiery red pepper piled in a mound. Each soldier grabs a handful and sprinkles it over his meal! Or at a Sikh regiment langar, a canister of pure Ghee, to ladle over it! The very common "Khadi chawal" is one dish that shows influences. The regiments from the south will always flavor it with coconut, in thin gravy, the Dogra's with "Kachalus" (type of potatoes), and the Punjabis with flaming red taraka and coriander. The Langar cuisine sometimes influences the kitchens and "pack food" of the entire regiments too. "Pooran Puri" an elaborate dish from Maharastra is one such example. Made to last for days, it is carried as dry ration when the units are on military exercises. Langar food sometimes influences the Menus of the Officers mess too. Young officers who have just come into the Army and Battalions have to stay with the troops for some time. Eating from the Langar becomes unforgettable and sometimes a memory that prompts them to demand "Langar type Khadi or mutton!"

But Divya was not thinking of all that or even wanting to learn anything kept her mind angry. Finally she made her way out to join her husband and leave for the party. They arrived at the venue. Lights sparkled and music played. "I love the way we live every moment-you never know when things turn and seriousness takes over our routines." Prakash commented hearing the loud music.

They sat down to witness an entertainment program. The program was so simple and loud in its representation that it had the entire audience in an uproar of merriment! Divya, seeing the gaudy garish representations, followed by the delicious langar food and the joyful interaction, was often forgetting to keep her grumpy expressions. But she wanted to teach Prakash a lesson. Make him feel sorry for her. She was so jumbled in her attitude that she confused everything in her mind. That is why Divya still could not accept the warm bonhomie generating around. She still maintained the willful stubbornness to hold the feeling of an injured soul who was a victim here! Since she had almost joined in to the fun and would have *almost* admitted she was enjoying herself, later returning home she hardened her stance towards Prakash even more. He features remained cold and intolerant. When she lay under the covers in bed Divya was beginning to feel the pressure of this 'hate all' attitude. Deep down she was wondering how she would convince all this was not her or her lifestyle and be believed. As she sleepily dozed off an unchecked thought told her, "admit defeat and join in....!" she had no time to process this thought since she slipped into deep slumber by then.

The next morning, Divya woke up angry that she had even thought of admitting her attitude was wrong. Today she was supposed to accompany Shivi and Fatima to a village adopted by the Army under project "Sadbhawana."

This school had been started for the village children and as a welfare measure, taking turns, the ladies from the forces went and helped supervise this.

When the ladies came to take her, Divya was so cold that they decided to leave her alone. In the confines of the vehicle this was getting really awkward, but Divya seemed not to care. She stared out of the window and sulked for reasons she herself was now beginning to find difficult to process!

They had to travel really far to get to the remote area. Midway there was a coffee and sandwiches break. Divya did not eat anything. She refused with an edge of superior insolence tingeing her refusal! In fact just managing to stay within the polite parameters of verbal interaction!

However, Divya could not quite keep her attention to herself. More then once she caught herself absorbing the scenic landscapes undulating outside the car windows. It was so beautiful.

The school, an unassuming building stood on a hillock. Below was a natural pond that glistened and shone at the distance they stared below from. The air was fresh and healthy. A slight breeze ruffled their hair as they walked to the school.

Children from neighboring villages were there too. However these village schools had very few students. Parents hereabouts mostly did not want to educate their children. The wanted to enlist their children into their own occupations like farming, tea gardens etc, schooling and education in their mind was actually a waste of time and did not serve any purpose in their way of life!

Now with the motivation of the Army and other government bodies some sort of awareness was slowly spreading.

Climbing the incline to reach the school building, Divya noticed the children present, sitting and studying in a classroom through a huge grill-less window. A teacher was loudly chanting tables.

She was surprised to know that this school just had one functional classroom as of now! Fatima and Shivi were talking and she overheard this bit of information.

"It is one classroom now, but we hope to motivate the parents hereabouts and see these schools grow!"

Fatima and Shivi had brought free books, pencils, crayons and lots of paper. The Principal of this small school welcomed them warmly. After the distribution, leaving them, Divya walked towards edge of the slope and sat down on a rock.

"She is actually quite stubborn!" Fatima whispered catching the fact that Divya had distanced herself from them and was sitting alone outside.

"Ssssh! Lito ma am said we have to be patient." Shivi admonished mildly.

Fatima rolled her eyes shrugging.

They were planning to sit with a class for a drawing class. The entire school had about twenty five children in all, so all classes sat together with them.

Divya, after some time became restless. She turned and stared into the grill-less window. The children were seemingly having a fun time with Shivi and Fatima. For a moment Divya felt her resolve to remain unaffected slipped and she looked yearningly at them, should she...?

But a voice inside her head shouted a big "NO!" Imagine the humiliation admitting you are wrong!

Actually, Divya herself did not understand her own attitude. The entire stance she had taken was tiring her now. But somewhere she felt that since she was in this back of beyond place she was missing some earth changing happenings back in the city. The new fashions, new places everything was out of reach because she was here. This thought maddened her. I refuse to be drawn into this silly life...I..hate this stupid place...I hate all this....!

But somehow she seemed to be convincing herself more then anything. With a determined twist, Divya turned her body around so her back was to the window.

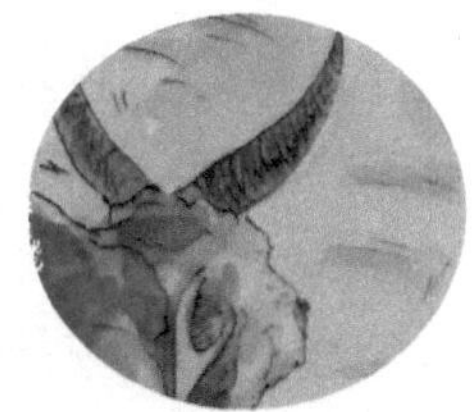

A conference was on in the OPS (Operations) room. A general sense of urgency filled the room since a small operation had been concluded successfully between suspected militants and a patrol party. Though the operation took place some miles away, it was being monitored from the OPS room.

"Yes, yes, good!" Col Kher nodded and finished his conversation over the radio set. The phone rang again and this time it was Raj returning from the location of the alleged skirmish.

"Raj and his men have met up with some suspicious characters, they are returning now, just call the local police chap here and inform him that we are bringing in two miscreants." Col Kher told his adjutant.

Raj stared at the two ruffians and asked in a steely voice, "do you have weapons?"

The two vigourously shook their heads.

"Then why did you run away when you saw the Army vehicles approach?"

Earlier Raj was leading a patrol. The road was flanked by endless fields with high grass. Raj had just conducted a search in the early hours of the morning. A group of doubtful characters hiding in a hut had been apprehended. After they had been handed over to the local authorities, Raj was returning to the unit. Earlier, just as they sped down the roads two men on the sides suddenly emerged from the high grass and began to balefully stare at the green vehicles. One of them then took out a mobile phone and began to speak into it pointing at the vehicles. Raj's keen eyes caught this in the rearview mirror and he immediately braked. Reversing the vehicle he stopped by them. Their faces drained of colour and they turned to flee. But with quick reflexes Raj caught them.

"Why were you pointing and gesticulating towards our vehicles and speaking into the phone? Is there an ambush up ahead on the mountain paths perhaps?"

The men looked down and said nothing.

Raj sighed and asked one of the soldiers'

to put them into the back of one of the vehicles.

This was all a part of their job. As a soldier, Raj and his unit sleeplessly followed leads and clues towards any trouble elements disturbing the peace of the nation and off course now these borders. Constant vigil against threats in these sensitive areas made up for the entire days work for the men in olive green. Raj pensively stared out of the window and saw a QRT (quick reaction team) patrolling the sides of the roads. "Sigh! these men will not think twice of giving up their lives for the call of duty-I salute them." His thoughts were interrupted by Captain Prakash who was sitting with him.

"Er sir...I..want to apologize

"What for?"

"Last evening---er Divya was.."

"Aww come off it-forget it we understand- whoaaa!"

Suddenly with a jerk the driver braked. In apparent rightful authority to do just that, an elephant stood in the middle of their path! Benchmark rules intoned that all wild life had a right to pass first. If stopped by a herd of elephants one needed to make a quiet escape quickly, since they could be very unpredictable. A lone elephant was in-fact even more dangerous. So the sensible action would be to turn around and actually flee, without being noticed! "Go on the opposite of where the wind is blowing so the elephant does not catch your smell." Was the general course of action recommended in such situations.

With bated breath, emitting an undercurrent of tension within the confines of the vehicle, the driver slowly backed.

"Wait." Raj interjected suddenly.

"Sir-Raj sir....what the...?" Captain Prakash blurted.

The driver stopped the vehicle and Raj jumped out.

"Sir-not wise to do that....!" But Raj had already left!

To the fascination of the present onlookers, Raj walked up right to the elephant and said in a gentle voice, "hello Dumpu."

Dumpu swayed and tinkled; then with a gentle touch of his trunk nuzzled Raj.

"I thought I recognized those bells and

anklets! There you go old boy!" Raj petted the pachyderm.

Dumpu tried to find something to eat in Raj's shirt pocket.

"Ha ha ha!" Raj guffawed.

By now Captain Prakash also came forward.

A crackling sound in the undergrowth announced the presence of Dasuda, who emerged from the surrounding fields.

"Aha Saab-so Dumpu recognized you!"

"So it seems Dasuda!"

"In fact we were just at the village-Tinku baby was with us. Her mother called her for lunch, so the two of us, still energetic and not willing to rest walked here...to these fields.."

Dasuda smiled then added, "I don't know how much these fields will last though!"

"Why do you say that?"

"Old man's instinct. I talk more for my *saab's* tea plantation. The location is bad."

"Yes there is always some talk about that is there not?"

"Yes. Sometimes the storms are bad-so far we have been lucky, but if we have unprecedented rains, we shall be flooded."

Raj and Prakash viewed the geography of the place they stood.

"I am sure you have had rains before; how old is the plantation?" Raj squinted his eyes and asked.

"Saab not very old-and somehow the rains have been kind. But old Binka at the village is predicting disaster this time. See." They followed his pointing finger. "See that high hill, it has sliding lands that have borne the onslaught of rains remarkably till now. Yet if there is pressure as of now... no less than a deluge can be predicted." He announced. "This whole track that covers from that point, Sen gardens and those villages are in the danger zone. Huge rain catchment bowls have naturally developed. However streams and tributaries seem to burst into an overflow if any very heavy rain fall occurs! Yes, we do get our share of overflows, but they have been manageable so far--thankfully nothing untoward has happened but..."

"Binka?" Raj cocked an eyebrow in query.

"Oh he is like a village astrologer – and one time worker in the weather department! He predicts rains, and good, bad fortunes.

He sits at the big branch tree at the village and wails that the world is ending!" Dasuda chuckled.

"But Mr Sen, his gardens are on hilly slopes then..?" Prakash asked.

"Sir most tracts are low lying. Only the house is built on higher ground. Anyhow lets hope Binka's crazy warnings bear no fruit."

Raj just shrugged and nodded a goodbye. Soon they army vehicle was back on road heading to the battalion.

Raj, later in the early evening, was taking an evening run when he heard the first clap of thunder. An unease settled in his heart, but he shook it off.

"Pshaw what is wrong with me-how can an old man's blathering affect me!" Raj ran harder. The thunder actually brought no rain. A heavy breeze gathered and actually carried any rain clouds away.

After his run Raj drove his vehicle to the Sen's plantation. He had fixed up a game of squash with Mr Sen at the tea planters club that was in another plantation, some miles away. Mr Sen met him at the gates of the club. The huge white columned edifice of the club was reminiscent of the British Raj days. It had an understated lingering atmosphere. Automatically one spoke in low tones so as to not disturb the peacefully environs! They walked towards the changing rooms. Swinging his duffel bag, Raj admired the ye old charm of the club. He smiled when he crossed the cards room where a huge sign said, SILENCE ZONE, PLAYERS ARE PLAYING!

They walked past little sitting rooms, the swimming pool area and finally reached the courts.

Entering the changing room, Raj switched his shoes to ones that were more appropriate for squash. Wearing white tees and shorts Raj looked quite toned and well muscled. Seeing him Mr Sen commented, "you army fellows are so fit!"

"We school ourselves to be fit!" Raj chuckled.

"I know-but I cannot follow such exercise routines for the life of me. How do you do it?"

"The right attitude I guess?" Raj shrugged.

They had reached the squash courts by now.

Squash is a vigorous game. Soon it upped the ante on Raj's fitness as opposed to Mr Sen who was soon scrambling to keep up!

"Huff puff offfff!" Raj this time I shall beat you...ugh...offof... not fair you take the game away always!" Mr Deb Sen chased the ball around the court virtually at Raj's bidding. With a faultless flick Raj pushed the ball with a strong whack that send Deb running forward. Another flick sent him backwards. Soon strong swear words, shots as the tiny squash ball zinged off the walls and groans interpreted the tempo of the game. Finally it was over and Deb and Raj strolled up to the club cafeteria for iced tea and cakes. "How do you manage 'squash' victory all times Raj?" Deb asked, his broad smile taking away the sting of his abrupt words.

" Ha ha ha! Just perfected my game that is all!"

"We all are going to be flooded and we shall perish." Came up a child's voice behind them. Startled Raj glanced behind to see Shaila Sen and Tinku joining them. Tinku said the words. She stood next to them and once again ominously repeated them.

"Tinku enough. That is very rude." Shaila admonished. Deb dropped to his knees so he could be at Tinku's eye level, "Don't say such things."

"But Baba that is what Dasuda and Binka say-we must listen."

"Rubbish-it is all rubbish. No flood will hit us I assure you." Deb dismissed her warnings as he sprang up.

"Hello Major Raj." Shaila nodded with a warm smile.

"Hello Major Raj." Tinku too parroted.

Laughing Raj turned to Tinku, "I met Dumpu today."

"Oh you did?" Came Tinku's clipped response. "I am glad."

Just then the Deb's colleagues joined them. Suddenly they were surrounded by children and their mother's too who had accompanied their husband's. Tinku dashed about calling to Mitsy and Neha to follow her out.

"She is always the leader!" Deb smiled as he saw his daughter leave with a small entourage.

"Yes." Raj agreed. "By the way Deb, this warnings of floods and low lying area your garden is in don't' you think you should take precautions?"

"I know I bought this garden cheap because of this reason. It is small and my life's savings have gone into it. But I am not going to run scared because of some silly predictions from an unreliable source."

Raj was quiet. Deb changed the topic and soon they were discussing the latest model of racing cars and the cricket scores. Driving back Raj did not really think of floods and slides, he in fact was planning his intent to wake up early and photograph the sun breaking into early morning.

The next morning, Raj crunched through the foliage. Narrowing his eyes he identified the perfect spot. Focusing his camera he began to shoot. The sun splintered into the sky lighting it into variant hues. Lazily it rose, peeping from stray clouds and a clear sky at the human clicking away! Yes, bending low Raj clicked away. Soon he realized that he had captured the beauty of the moment. He sighed and flopped down right where he was standing. He had moved some distance from the unit area and come to a vast clearing. Climbing over a small rocky patch Raj had stationed himself to watch the sun rise. Now pulling out his coffee thermos, which he wisely carried, he poured some coffee and slowly sipped the liquid still enjoying the moments he had managed to be in even though it was 3.00 AM! Today is our cross country run. Hmm that should be interesting since I can get the gist of the place. Beyond the river provided the perfect sound tracks to the early morning chirping of the birds. Birds! What a delightful variety he spotted here. His camera kept clicking when he had freshly arrived. Raj even spotted some vividly coloured birds hopping on the trees. I should study names of birds and gain knowledge about them. He lazily thought. Hmmm add the write up behind each snap I click of them....Here orchids flowers grew in abundance. Literally plucked off trees. Cane, bamboo furniture was very popular too. Raj stretched then lay back still enjoying the quietude.

Some months back he had tried to catch the daily routine of a wild buffalo on his camera. This buffalo grazed all alone in

an empty field. He apparently had strayed away from his herd. The buffalo made a beautiful picture since hues of brown orange and gray flushed as a background in the changeling evening sky. So enraptured was Raj that he parked his jeep and crept up close to get good photographic shots. "Click click click!" his camera went. Oh oh bad idea. The buffalo was irritated. He balefully turned to glare at Raj. This way the Buffalo took in a waft of a human present by smell! Hmmm Raj did not get the hint. Sigh. Buffalo decided to chase him away. His head pointed towards Raj, the buffalo charged!

Raj knew the buffalo could out run him too! *The jeep suddenly seemed unreachable!* He did some tactics. Every time Raj ran he ran around in circles then resumed his run towards the jeep. He had no idea whether this would work. It seemed to have- the buffalo following him by smell did the circles before resuming the chase-thus initiating some delay! Raj then actually threw off his tee shirt to stall the Buffalo. This was difficult since the camera slung over his shoulder hampered him. But he managed to tear the tee off! He flung it over his shoulder. The Buffalo reached the tee shirt. He stopped. His horns lifted it up. Then he smelled it. With an angry grunt he attacked it. The buffalo stabbed the tee brutally! "Yikes that could be me!" Raj thought. Oh oh the Buffalo abruptly realized the ruse. Angry and fuming the Buffalo charged again! The best thing would have been to climb a tree. But Raj could not see one. It was a freak chance that the Buffalo did not catch up with him! Raj was nearing the jeep. "Come on come on!" He was in the jeep turning the ignition. With a roar the jeep started!

"Whoaaaaaaaaaaaaaaaaaaaaaaaaaaaaa aaaaaaaaaaaaaaaaa!" Raj drove away! He was bare- chested since his tee shirt was a shredded mess on that field! The buffalo chased after him in the jeep for a long way. Even now Raj burst into a silent laugh when he thought of his quick silver geta-way!

After a while Raj decided to return to his Mess rooms. He had jogged all the way from the Mess. Raj loved to run and this place provided all he needed for that! Sprinting ahead, he reached the Cant limits. Squinting he realized a lady was walking in great agitation up and down one housing enclave. "Who is up so early I wonder?" As he neared he realized it was Divya. She looked furious and as if she had been crying. "Morning Ma'am!" Raj called out but did not stop as he sprinted past her. She barely answered his greetings. Oh oh I think the two have fought again! Raj surmised, great pity –they don't seem to be working this out at all!

•••

That morning, whilst Raj was on his photography adventures, Tinku awoke very early and ran out. She was allowed to do as she pleased as long as she remained within the set boundaries her parents had laid out for her. Reaching Dumpu, she immediately climbed the rickety platform. Raising her sweet voice she sang songs and picked ou from the bunch of flowers she was carrying and stuck them into Dumpu ears. She was standing on the high platform from which she was conveniently at shoulder level with Dumpu. "Dumpu you look so beautiful….!" Tinku then dipped her hands into chalk power and streaked designs over Dumpu's Back. Soon Tinku was joined by two of her friends, Mitsy and Neha, who had arrived from the neighboring gardens. Dumpu became a part of their tea party! Tinku decided to take her friends for a ride on Dumpu. Dasuda accompanied them. Dumpu followed a track into the jungle area. Overhead monkeys screeched when the small tea party ambled into their space. Dasuda led them into a clearing. The girls jumped off. "See!" Tinku pointed to butterflies over a patch of flowers. Her friends squealed in delight. Dismounting, they ran to chase the butterflies. Dumpu just stood and watched them. One would actually feel his happiness of being there. Later Dasuda led them towards the natural waterfall. Dumpu with his passengers walked right into the fall to bathe! Soon they were plunged into the shallow pond from where the stream in rivulets found an out.

Tinku began to imagine she was an underwater diver. She started to play a game of dive and lift with Dumpu. She would dive into the pond and Dumpu would snake his trunk into the water find her and lift her up. "Mitsy, Neha see.... owwww whoooo!" Tinku squealed every time Dumpu lifted her and placed her gently one the side. Soon Mitsy Neha joined into this game. Howls of laughter filled the air!

"Wheeeeeeeeee!" the children splashed and played after the 'game'. Dumpu now and then sprayed them with his trunk!

The water fall was actually like a natural shower cubicle. The waters flowed off an edge into a small pond below. It was perfectly safe to be there. In fact Dumpu mostly came here to cool himself during the intense summer months. "Splosh...... splishhhhh!" Rain marked its presence suddenly; without warning a shower of rain splattered from the skies. Dasuda quickly collected his charges and urged them to return home. Giggling and laughing the girls atop Dumpu, crooned and sang as they reached home.

●●●

Raj after that eventful morning with his photography ran back to the Mess rooms deciding to catch more photographs in the afternoon. Thus it was later in the day, after work he decided to sit atop the natural boulders overlooking the river to take more photographs.

"Sploshhhh!" One fat drop trickled on to Raj's face. He looked up. That one drop shook him out of his reverie. The skies without warning had darkened. The sun had slipped away. The unexpected rain, which suddenly came down in torrents following that one drop had Raj scrambling up. Jamming his camera into its bag Raj sprinted back. A huge clap of thunder erupted. "Ayaaaaaa-WHOOOOPII come on now ha ha ha ha!" Raj let out a war cry and a whoop still trying to outrace the wet showers bearing down on him so un-expectantly. He reached his rooms drenched. Laughing and highly amused Raj toweled down and went in for a shower.

•••

Her friends had left. Tinku sat near the long French windows and stared at dismay as the rain poured down. She was so worried. Somehow in her bones she felt things were not right. Then she recalled Binka's warnings and her stomach churned more. In her mind she felt Dumpu was helpless. Ever since Dumpu had been domesticated Tinku felt sad. Since he had been away from his wild brethren too long!

Comments that were passed about always said how wild animals when domesticated lost their natural instincts! They were more likely to get into trouble then their free and savage counterparts.

Tinku suddenly stood up. Clambering down the creaky wooden doors she rushed into the kitchens. The cooks were stirring up a storm. "Arre Tinu baba feeling hungry?" Asked Shomir, the older cook looking up from the pot he was stirring. Chuckling he boomed, "today much cooking is happening. Saab wants only soup, madam wants an entire meal of fish and rice with vegetable, you have asked for pasta and pizza...aaaah my hands are going crazy cooking, cooking for my family eh?"

Tinku giggled and climbed on to the counter top, via a high chair placed near it. Shomir chopped up a fresh pineapple and arranged it on a plate for her. Chomping the juicy pineapple Tinku said, "Shomir da er...the story of the er floods, um ...!" Tinku somehow could not ask about the horrible stories of the so called impending disaster since she feared it so much herself that bringing to an open verbal thought scared her.

But Shomir understood at once. Now being from the village and not averse to airing his own fears, Shomir somehow found a vent to talk things out. So Tinku with growing nervousness amongst the spicy hot smells emitting from his cooking heard the story of how his entire village had been devastated by the floods years ago.

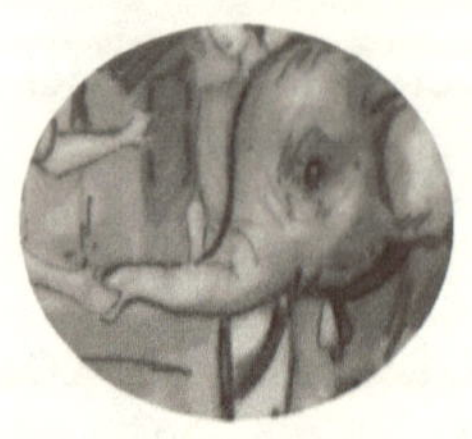 

It rained and rained and rained subsequently. The Cant area hardly showed any reaction to that since the roads were on high-ground and drainage excellent. All the same continuous rain can always be a damper.

The activities of course went on as usual. So much so the cross country run also continued as scheduled. Raj did not mind the wet at all. Running with his men and taking arduous tracks challenged him. Seeing through the rain was a matter of practice too. Map reading, finding directions, was supposed to be done by picking up natural indications and landmarks, so said their training. Raj and his contingent ran across certain landscapes marked down as the route. The huge gushing tributary of the river was their guideline. They ran up the thick mountain routes with precise timing and trained breathing tactics. It was on their return at Noon that Raj decided to jog a bit more. He asked the contingent to return to the unit whereas he decided to exercise and do some yoga/gymnastic moves in-spite of the down pour!

Raj was completely alone on those paths now. He stood on a knoll and could see his men going smaller and smaller as they sprinted back to the unit lines.

"Aaaaah!" Raj loudly took some sharp breaths. He began to affect some Kung Fu moves. Kicking sharply in the air and punching his hands forward Raj exercised. His exercise veered into yoga soon. So when calamity struck Raj was actually standing on his head observing landscapes. Suddenly the rainy skies became pitch dark. MMMMMMMMMMMMMMMMMMMMM MMMMKAMKAK!"

A terrible tearing sound blanked out all other noises in and around the area. Raj straightened and jumped up to stand all at once.

Raj stopped and turned around. "Oh my God! Watch out!" Raj looped up from the upside down mode he was in and shouted as a huge gush of water breaking through the trajectory above slammed him and rolled him on with unimaginable force. Raj was pushed forward. Trying to grip something tightly to stop himself Raj had no control over his limbs. The river and the roads seemed to merge into one strain. He felt himself being pulled under in the rush of waters. "Flash floods" was his last thought as he went under.

"Thank God schools are shut and we do not have to send the kids off in this rain!" Commented Savitri as she tried out a new recipe she had got from Fatima. It was a 'yakini briyani' recipe. Savitri stirred the pot when the screen door at her kitchen was knocked. It was her neighbour Priya, "Hi! Just came over to ask you to give me some ideas. Binny (her daughter) has a school play coming up when school reopens, she needs to dress like a princess...yum what are you cooking?"

Savitri grinned, "You can sample it when t is made...." Their conversations later veered to Divya's behavior. "I don't understand why Mrs Kher tolerates it. For me I really am thinking of not calling her to participate in any thing...what a sulky woman. Prakash is such a nice boy..." They chatted for a while then as they moved to the living room a loud crash startled them. "Oh no what is that????" Savitri startled and scared all at once shouted. Priya stood stock still in shock. To their horror the room suddenly lost all lights.

It became pitch dark and another huge rumble shook the foundations of their block. "Yeowwwwwww! Earthquake? Oh my gosh what is that??????" the ladies squealed abruptly sensing all was not right although not quite understanding what was happening.

The two were petrified since all the shaking and rumble made them feel very vulnerable all of a sudden.

Her children ran into the room. She gathered them around. Priya's children ran in too. They all were so scared...

•••

Lito stopped in her tracks. "What was that sound. Why is it so dark? Oh no ....?!? She worriedly ran to the window and stared out. Snuggy –Woo even though so huge was trembling like a leaf due to the thunders. Lito petted and calmed him. Finally she allowed the shivering dog to climb the forbidden armchair. He settled in happily. Lito put on some music and tried to become calm herself too!

The rain curtained off any vision, with relief she saw her husband enter after two hours of tense speculation. "What was that-what is happening? The rain is sounding horrible..."

"Sweetheart listen to me, don't panic, our area is safe. Our location is at the curve, which naturally acts like a drain-plus this Cant is made very sensibly... but we need to swing into rescue action. Raj is still out though his boys returned....and there has been a terrible landslide accompanied by flash floods. I need to organize boats and marry up with the civil authorities who have not stopped phoning for help.

Suddenly the phone pealed. Lito rushed to pick up Savitri's call. "Don't panic it is ok...it is just a storm ...a bad storm....what? The kid's are scared....ok lets all meet up at the Mess...we can have lunch and be together whilst the storm rolls over...um um...ok come on let us meet up!"

Lito turned to her husband, "we shall be

together since the kids are getting restless.."

"Good idea since we are going to be a while...!" Col Kher nodded and exited quickly.

•••

When Lito sent out the messages to meet at the Mess every one complied quickly. They knew it was better to be together since this turn in weather was confusing. Savitri collected the ladies and kids on her block and made her way to the mess. She swallowed her fears of the terrible weather conditions, surrounding them and concentrated on keeping the kids occupied within the big vehicle. Luckily a unit vehicle was picking all of them up. They had to make a slow progress to the Mess, which was otherwise quite near. However the rain was pounding down in solid torrents that made vision near impossible!

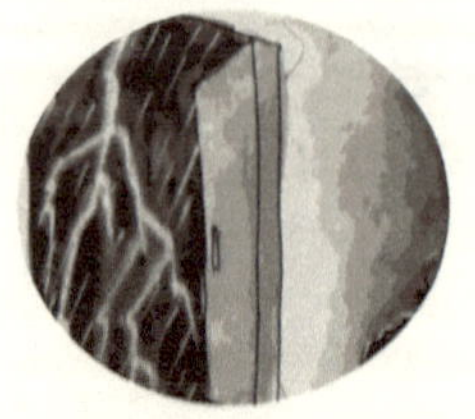

10

Divya frowned as she stared out of the window. The weather was horrible and what was that blaring cracking sound? Oh no it is raining. There is a storm exploding. Oh I am alone. Where is Prakash??

Hating to admit it she was worried since her husband Prakash had still not returned from his games time. She sat in the living room on a sofa and began to sulk. Her sulk grew to anger and by the time a vehicle honked outside she was seething and furious.

"What?" she rudely asked the driver standing at her doorstep. The rain was creating a noisy din behind him.

Her disappointment increased by the fact it was not her husband.

"Ma am all ladies are requested to come to the mess for lunch. Mrs Kher has requested. Phone lines are now down so she could not call."

Squinting her eyes in anger and just short of snapping, Divya growled, "Tell Mrs Kher thank you but I am fine over here."

"But Ma am…"

Without a word Divya slammed the door.

Now that was extremely unforgivable. The poor driver had made his way her through horrible weather conditions. There were other already waiting in the vehicle. But Divya driven almost insane that Prakash was busy elsewhere was in some angry zone that the niceties of being polite excaped her totally.

Savitri was so angry at her attitude but did not want to display her rancor in front of others. When the driver conveyed Divya's message she just nodded and once again they painstakingly made their way to the Mess.

It was a great relief to all once they reached the Mess.

"Hi "Lito greeted her and the others warmly. "I really hope all is well but according to Col Kher there is a deluge erupting down there," she generally pointed out of the window towards Sen gardens. "He says we are safe this side but since they are on rescue duties we all can be together and not worry…" Soon the place was warm and cheerful. It distracted them from the bad weather unfolding outside. Lito was also informed that the Jawans wives had gathered at one place too and were playing "tambola" to pass time.

"Where is Divya?" Lito asked Savitri

"Madam declined your invite." Savitri sarcastically conveyed,

Lito chewed her lower lip but refrained from commenting. Instead she walked to the window and parted the curtains slightly. Her heart sank seeing the torrent outside. She send up a silent prayer hoping that everyone would remain safe and the weather would calm down.

Raj came to his senses underwater and almost immediately with dominant strokes surfaced. The currents of the river and the creation of the flash flood river ensued into a very dangerous situation indeed. Raj moved his legs in a continuous paddle trying to stay afloat. I need to get out of this river, Raj decided. He bobbed uncontrollably forward. His alert senses suddenly caught sight of something. Raising his hands with a strong force, Raj grabbed the tree branch overlooking the river. With a powerful heave, he pulled upwards. He grappled the bark and the branch he tightly held and managed to crawl higher. Sitting on his perch Raj skimmed the waters he had pulled out off below. "Oh my gosh this is bad!" Water was everywhere. Flooding and rising waters all that came in its way. The routes they had just run across on had drowned. "This tree will drown soon if the rain does not stop."

Raj muttered.

"Where am I?" Raj began to assess his whereabouts. The rain was so intense that it was impossible to see anything. Raj peered into the deluged landscape. He could not make out anything. I have to find a high ground and get out of here. Raj looked to his left and made out land, not drowned by the floods. With one forceful plunge Raj jumped off the tree and dived into the raging waters he pushed against the currents till his arms ached. But the flood and flow was ruthless Raj found himself suddenly hitting into the pitfalls unseen by the cover of water. Even as he swam and fought the currents, he was hit soundly by something! It was a frightened Antelope! The Antelope still had the rope he may have been tethered with around his neck. Struggling to stay afloat the Antelope desperately clawed the waters. In fact his hoof just missed Raj by inches. Raj had to help it. But he also was aware of the dangers of trying to help a panicked Antelope in these wild waters! Raj with some inhuman strength heaved himself and caught the rope and pulled forward still scissoring his legs fast so as to not drown.

The Antelope already in a senseless panic tried to gore, kick, push and hit Raj all at once! Luckily the rushing waters stalled any brutal attacks effectively!

Also, Raj forced his way forward moving away from target range! The Antelope twisting and turning behind him somehow remained afloat too!

"Cough.....glug....cough I see a bank!" Raj generally shouted!

He managed to reach the bank. "Aaaaaah-----offfff...cough cough hang in there old crazy Antelope I will pull you out!" Raj shouted. Not letting go of the rope he scrabbled over. Pinning his heels deep into the muddy edges he pulled the Antelope. Helped to some extent by the propelling waters the Antelope bumped into the bank and with some glimmer of reasoning climbed out! Raj quickly let go off the rope and "whooooooa watch it!" moved aside for the alarmed mammal to blindly race towards the higher grounds in this unending sheets of rain. "And you are most welcome!" Raj shouted after the receding back of the Antelope!

I have reached high ground. Intently observing his surroundings Raj got his bearings. He was out of the water now and he realized his unit was just a little further away. When Raj reached the unit he was met with a flurry of activities.

The catchment areas, which acted like natural reservoirs had burst! The fury of the rains and this happening ensued into a flash flood. A shift in landmass included a terrible landslide too!

The danger increased when these waters joined the river Brahmaputra's tributaries that flowed in these vicinities! The swollen tributaries, rains and catchment waters created a deluge.

"Thank God you are safe!" Col Kher boomed on seeing Raj.

Raj had quickly managed to go to his rooms and change before joining the rest at the office.

Without waiting for an answer Col Kher informed him, "we are assisting the civil authorities with rescue operations. I have immediately arranged boats. But boats can only ply in the low lying areas."

Raj nodded assimilating the instructions.

"However up above the flash floods are so bad that going there is insane. Get out there...save people, its mayhem!" Alok Kher announced to all and sundry in the room.

Without thought for any dangers the soldiers went into a rescue drill.

The rescue boats were careening down the waters. Of course boats could only ply in the low lying areas. The soldiers fished out people fleeing the raging floods above. Cries for help filled the air. The soldiers safely transported the displaced residents. The waters were rising and the situation fraught with dangers. The soldiers worked tirelessly. The rain just did not stop. This was not good since rain was abetting the swell of the flash flood waters. Mudslides and the landslide cut off most of the vicinities in the path of this flood. This could trigger a massive earthquake? Was a silent thought amongst many. Then there would be an even worse disaster! A silent prayer that the situation would hold was on most lips.

Raj jumped on to one boat. The boatman negotiated his boat downstream with expertise. The boat was like a canoe. The boat man stood paddling with a long stick.

He was a regular boatman out to help. Army boats were plying too. The boatman managed to reach the Sen plantation. Here Raj jumped off. With quick strides he reached the house. Evacuation was in full swing. Suddenly a cry of anguish held Raj's attention. "Tinku....Tinku...Tinku!" It was only when Raj reached Deb Sen that he incorporated the fact with horror. Tinku Sen was missing.

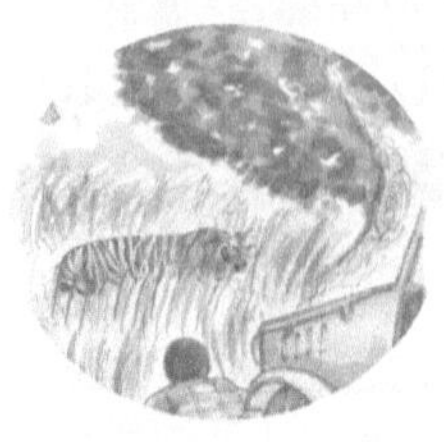 

Earlier...

The entire day Tinku had nervously observed the weather take a turn from bad to worse. She had even tried to take matter in her own hands by leaving through the back door and go to Dumpu to make sure he was safe. Of course she was roundly caught and not allowed.

"Dumpu, please be safe!" Tinku murmured now and then. She tightly shut her eyes. Suddenly a vivid impact and a terrible vision of a scared and helpless Dumpu drowning flashed in her mind.

Dark mournful stories of floods had kept her worried for days. Now when it had happened she was petrified that Dumpu may drown or be swept away. In her childish mind she thought if she was with Dumpu she could guide him home. All the stories of the awful outcomes of flash floods crowded her mind. Her

stomach churned in tension. In a snap she decided to go looking for her beloved pet. Sometimes it is alright to take matter in your own hands. Mommy is busy ,Dad hardly believes me, so Dumpu, I have to save you from any calamity myself! Tinku firmly convinced herself. With this driving thoughts she raced down the wooden corridors of her home towards the back entrance. She ignored her parents shouts calling her. Her clattering footfalls had alerted them. But even before they could react Tinku had pushed open the door and was out. The din outside was loud. But in the cover of the porch things still did not seem so threatening. Dumpu is at the back. Tinku with this thought ran from the porch around the house. "Dumpu, Dumpu, Dumpu!" Tinku called but got no response. The slashing rains did not deter her. Tinku was so intent in finding her pet that she pushed ahead. But when she reached the knoll gradient she was propelled so hard by combination of rain, wind and noise that she stopped. For a moment the raging weather and rising waters stalled her next move, then with a small tumble she turned to go when her foot slipped badly. "Aaaaaaaahhhhhh!" Tinku rolled down the slope into the swirling waters below. Within seconds the currents flounced into action. Tinku felt herself pushed and with one powerful thrust she was swept into the flooding waters. Tinku paddled her hands and feet as fast as she could. Raising her head above the waters she yelled, "Dumpu.... Dumpu !" Tinku Sen had left safety to assure herself about Dumpu's welfare. Tinku never realized the enormity of the deluge. She unthinkingly had set out as the lone rescue party for her beloved pet.

14

"Deb calm down-what do you mean she is missing?" Deb turned a tortured expressions towards Raj and croaked, "she is nowhere... we cannot find her.....I am so scared.... she ...we heard her running out but we miscalculated thinking she had gone out from the front. The noise from the rain and storm confused us. We just could not find her!" Since the house was at a height it was not really flooded. However the tension was palpable. Tinku was missing. Dasuda stood in the kitchen fretting horribly. Raj calmed him. "Saab where could she have gone?" He wiped his eyes then said, "I know she went after that elephant. Dumpu ran away at the first clap of thunder...Tinku has been so worried...I should have realized her childish concerns were real...oh!"

Shaila was sobbing in a corner. The servants walked around in a hushed way. Raj walked down the corridor into the backyard leading to the area where Dumpu usually was. The rain was in full fury. Raj walked out and reached an edgy plateau. When he walked to its extreme in the inclement weather he looked down and gasped. If Tinku in the rain had fallen off this slope she was in big trouble since Raj could clearly make out the dangerously rising waters merging with the river. Raj left the house and found a boat to take him down the flooded streams. In the boat were the tea workers who were being evacuated to higher grounds.

It was a difficult ride since they were going upstream. The boat rocked badly. The assembly inhabit ting the space had to hold on tight. En-route two people were pulled in too. Raj decided to leave. He wanted to find Tinku.

Raj tersely instructed the boatman to bring him closer the edge. With a clean dive he was back into the waters. With determined strokes he moved inwards into plantation. The rows of bushes were drowned by the onslaught on the waters. Raj identified a tree and directed himself towards it. Aiming it as his goal he swam towards it. With some acrobatic maneuvers he scrambled up the tree. Using it as a view point he gazed out. The rain did not help him much. Yet something unbelievable caught his eyes so distance away. With a gasp Raj jumped off the tree and swam towards the oddity he had just recognized.

Dumpu hid his face into the shrub. He never realized his back body was totally exposed. He wished the entire din caused by the storm would just vanish. When Dumpu heard the loud crash of thunder and the waters bursting through natural bunds his heart stopped. His memory took him back to the time his Mother had been trapped. These sounds translated to the same din that had occurred then. He shook and shivered. When the loud cracking sound boomed again, Dumpu was blind with fear. He had just come to the gardens. Now in senseless panic he bolted. The rain, the lightning and thunder added to his panic. His desperate need to find a safe haven propelled him far, far away from the gardens. Then for just a second he heard it. A faint sound coming from a great distance.

"Dumpuuuuuuuuuuuuuuuuuuuuuuuuuu!"

Dumpu left his shrub and followed the

voice. Yes, it was his much loved friend Tinku calling him.

•••

Raj had to swim quite a distance. Finally he reached a slushy, opening almost the entry towards the heavy jungles surrounding the place. He lofted himself up onto a much higher ground, which oddly had a natural drainage-thus the water flowed rather than stagnated! With a dash he went into the jungle. The ground was water ridden but not flooded. Squishing forward Raj stopped and said, "Hey Dumpu.....I saw you from there!" Raj drenched, slit eyed due to the downpour, beckoned over his shoulders.

But Dumpu was not returning any greeting. "Heeeeeeeeeeetrumppppppppppp!" With a loud trumpet he snaked his trunk forward and without permission picked up Raj and flung him over his back.

"Heeyyyyy!" Raj tried not to feel the indignity of suddenly being ingloriously thrown on the elephant's back. Dumpu almost ran with his passenger.

"Dumpu...hey....!" Raj tried to balance himself with difficulty trying not to fall.

"Where are we going heyyyyy!" Regardless

of overhead tree branches, splashy ground and incessant rain Dumpu ran. Finally he stopped. Raj straightened to get his bearings. Then he saw her. With Dumpu, Raj was on a higher ground.

Just beyond them, where the flooding waters converged with the river, Tinku Sen was clinging to the top of a conical structure that was actually the roof of a barn made at the rim of the river.

•••

Earlier Tinku had found herself unceremoniously pushed into flooding waters assaulting the gardens as always predicted due to its geographical outlay. The house stood high above. It took Tinku ten minutes to run towards the outside shed. But in the darkness she missed her foot hold and tumbled down the slope right into the waters. However with some strength she had pushed towards the edge where the shrubbery still held on. Dumpuuuuuuuuuuuuuuuuuuuuuuuuuuuu!" Tinku continued to yell. Even as she was struggling to get a foot hold. Then, Dumpu suddenly appeared out of nowhere. His trunk slid forward and he pulled her up. Tinku shouted in relief "Dumpu you are safe!"Rain water soaked Tinku through. She tried to open her eyes but that was seeminging impossible! Clinging to Dumpu she urged, "Take me home Dumpu , turn around…lets go home!" Dumpu was frightened and naturally confused. He ran the wrong way. "Dumpu turn around no-no-no this is not the way…turn around!" Tinku screamed. Dumpu seemed very unsettled he circled in one place before again and again. Tinku petted him and tried to calm him. That worked. Suddenly Dumpu swung about and ran, choosing the right direction.

Combating the rain and the crashing waters, Dumpu ran forward in some confusion.

"Ahhhhhhhhhhhhhhhhhhhhhhhhhhhh Dumpu watch out!" Tinku yelled as the elephant tripped. Dumpu did not foresee the mudslide under his feet when he tried to edge out of the fast filling fields. He kind of skidded and Tinku fell off and before anything she was swept away…Rolling and tumbling for what seemed a long time before Tinku crashed into the solid cement barn. She clung to it for dear life.

•••

The swollen river was not helping things at all! The barn was now drowned in the waters. The barn was also caught in the vortex of waters flowing in a chaotic fusion of currents that made reaching it near impossible. In a quirk of fate this point was upstream. No boat could go there.

So Tinku searching for Dumpu had actually been swept here. She had managed to cling to the barn roof in the rising waters. But how long the barn would hold up in the face of the pushing, pounding waters was anyone's guess. If the barn broke since the construction was such Tinku would roll into the rivers and be swept downstream into dangerous waters. Then saving her would be near impossible. Tinku felt the vibrations shaking the barn, cracking and crumbling concrete, its breaking noises drowned by the multitude of other sounds, deepened the seriousness.

Raj realized the gravity of the situation. He had to think carefully before he jumped in to save her. He surveyed his options. Raj acknowledged the thick bamboo tree placed at the edge that bent almost halfway across towards the barn. But getting to the tree was not easy. It also seemed to be holding on yet it being uprooted was a possibility very soon to be manifesting waterways! Raj suddenly knew what he had to do.

15

Tinku Sen was petrified. The battering waters pummeled her. Her arms were aching. Seeing Maj Raj beyond with Dumpu was a relief. But how long she could hold on was becoming a serious threat. Raj was stripping bamboo from a tree. What was he doing? He made quite a pile. Then the wafer thin bamboo strips were knotted together to make a long rope. Now Raj also had a safety hemp rope swung around one shoulder. He unraveled that and joined the bamboo strip roped with the hemp rope to extend it. Tying it firmly he handed one end to Dumpu. Dumpu immediately held it fast. With no seconds to lose Raj guided Dumpu to huge bamboo tree, "Dumpu I am going in!" Raj had tied the rope to his waist-one end was held by Dumpu. Taking a deep breath Raj jumped in. "Splashhh!" he plummeted into the waters that filled his ears and nose. "Glug- glug- glug!" Water enclosed Raj's senses. With one huge effort he pressed upwards to surface. The location almost resembled a boiling cauldron since this seemed to be the most furious point of the floods!

His initial target was the tree. Raj felt he could use the tree as an anchor and pull Tinku out. But the muddy swirling waters rejected him. "Wham!" Raj helpless fought the currents. Slammed, he was thrown up, down, sideways. His strong body just managing to resist the onslaught. Using all his muscle power he held on and pushed towards the tree. But this task seemed to be spiraling towards failure....With one haul, Dumpu pulled Raj back with the help of the bamboo rope. This was not going to work. Raj tripped up to the edge with great difficulty. Breathing heavily Raj said, "N-o... this is not working!"

# 16

Lito, at the Mess was slightly perturbed and irritated that Divya had refused to come and join them at the mess. The spacious Mess had become the center for all. Children gathered in the recreation rooms, beginning to play games, the women gossiped and talked incessantly. Waiters ran around serving refreshments. The rain drummed over the roof, providing an almost musical background rendition!

The coziness safeness of being together in this horrible weather permeated a sense of comfort.

"Mrs Kher, Mrs Kher!" Shivi one of the unit ladies came in great agitation towards her. With her was her nine years old daughter Joyti. Joyti was looking very uncomfortable and was breathing funnily too.

"Shivi calm down what is the matter?" Lito asked with some alarm.

"In my hurry to come here I picked up

the wrong inhaler! Oh Joyti's asthma may trigger and the inhaler she is carrying has almost finished-I need to get a fresh inhaler form my house!"

Liot immediately stood up and thought hard. The only recourse was to drive herself since it was clear the men-folk were very tied up helping out elsewhere. This to Lito's mind was too small an emergency to bother them with. As of now it also transpired that Lito was the only one whose car was at the Mess.

"Come on let us go and get it."

Shivi nodded to her daughter, "Kher aunty and I will go and fetch the inhaler, Joyti you wait here."

Lito and Shivi walked to the entrance door. Peeping out, Lito gasped, "the weather is really bad! Run, my car is parked in the porch itself!" Ducking to avoid the stray raindrops sprinkling from the open sides of the otherwise covered porch the two ran to the car. Lito drove very carefully through the rain swept roads. Biting her lower lip, she negotiated turns with utmost caution. Shivi sat stiff and nervously clenching and unclenching her hands. Her house was not very far however there was a sharp incline to be maneuvered before one reached the housing complex. The small car tediously took the gradient. "Come on, come on" Lito muttered. In the small confines of the car the two held on to their fears. The slashing rains were ineffectually swabbed by the wipers. Narrowing her eyes and trying to concentrate on the road ahead, Lito continued the nightmarish climb. Finally with a big sigh of relief they were at Shivi's house. Shivi wasted no time in getting the inhaler. Once again Lito carefully drove back. When they returned to the road below, Lito suddenly said, "Divya's house is at the end of this road-before turning to the mess lets just check on her...just five minutes!"

"But Mrs Kher, you send her a vehicle-she refused to come?!"

"So? I er feel responsible-it just does not seem fair leaving her alone ...I just feel it in my bones that I need to at least get her here to be with us...!" Lito's voice trailed as she continued to drive towards Divya's house.

"Who is that?" Shivi peered through the gushes of rain and pointed through the windscreen to the road ahead.

Through the rain clouded wind screen they espied someone fallen on the road. As recognition dawned, Lito gasped in horror,

"Oh my gosh is that Divya???"

•••

EARLIER...

Divya was seething since Prakash did not return home. She ranted and raged. Finally finding sitting at home impossible she emerged from her apartment and ran down the stairs into the garden. The staircase was soaked and slippery. It was raining so intensely that Divya was immediately wet but mindlessly she stormed out to the road. "Guess what-I am alone here....no one is around!" She also realized that there was no one around. Since the housing schemes had blocks of four apartments at some distances. Her mind took on all the drama she could contrive. "Here all alone I am-I will drench in this rain catch a fever and that will teach Prakash a lesson." She cooked up such a painful vision of her suffering and somehow that affecting Prakash to feel guilty that she walked up and down in the rain fuming.

"Ohhhhhh! I hate this place. The rain, the leeches, the ...the ooooohhhh! I will die here and it will serve him " Divya growled and sobbed feeling so sorry for herself. In utmost anger she swung around. Then it unexpectedly happened. When her foot slipped she had no idea but with a loud "swat" her one leg jackknifed up and with a loud crunch she hit the gravel on the roadside. She fell hard on her ankle.

"Owwwwwwww!" Divya screamed in agony. She tried to stand but the pain was crippling. Rain unsympathetically pounded her. "H-el---h-elp!" Divya whispered in a scared voice. But as she lay outside her house on the road unable to move she realized no one was around to help her.

"Groan...oh no this is so painful!"

Diviya whimpered holding on to her badly sprained ankle. She tried to sit up but the pain was so intense that it was impossible. Howling she cried for help. She was so involved in her grief and sorry situation she missed the headlights of a vehicle drawing up right next to her.

"Divya? What is the matter? Why are you here?"

Divya almost died of relief, "oh Mrs Kher am I glad to see you...I have ...my ankle..!"

Lito jumped off her car and ran to Divya; ignoring the rain. "I was so worried you are alone here I just decided to drive up to check!" Lito spoke loudly through the pounding rain. She helped Divya up who groaned. By now Shivi too jumped out and helped to pick Divya up.

"Come we are all at the Mess...the menfolk are out assisting with rescues...don't worry we will take care of you...." Lito assured Divya as she limped with help to the car. Thoroughly drenched by now they managed to help Divya into the car.

Divya stared at Lito-suddenly her body flushed with shame. Every rude comment, every boorish behaviour she had thrown towards this angelic lady crowded her mind. Her throat choked and she felt miserable. But her ankle allowed her no apologies to be said openly. She sat in mute pain as Lito drove them to the Mess. However, down the journey to the Mess ,her pain was becoming extra emotional rather then physical as she thought more and more about how mean she had been.

•••

It was then Raj thought of helicopters. The only way is to heave her off aerially. Swimming up can turn tables since the whirl of waters can suck us in. They could have pressed in Army helicopter services for the rescue. But he knew no helicopter would take off in this rain. The helicopter would be on standby duty. As soon as it was clear and feasible they would join the rescue teams.

The only way to confirm all this was to go to the helipad area. "Dumpu hurry take me to the helipad." As if Dumpu knew that! Raj almost forced Dumpu to carry him and Dumpu listened! He headed wherever Raj guided him by pushing his ears!

Urging him Raj steered the pachyderm to the helipad, which fortunately was not so far off.

With urgent pace Dumpu ran through the rainy terrain. It would not be wrong to say that a nightmare of a journey ensued. Dumpu ran through the battering rain, regardless of Raj clinging to his neck trying to focus on the directions. Alongside the stress of leaving Tinku still in the waters prevailed. Raj had to keep ducking so tree branches would not hit him as Dumpu pelted full throttle forward.

It was quite dramatic to see Raj running out from the jungle cover on an elephant. There was a posse of men and a helicopter on the helipad. They stopped in their tracks and stared. Further down there was a hangar like construction. A pilot emerged from there and he walked to the copter.

"Hey hey I need help...!" Raj jumped off Dumpu and rushed up to them. Seeing they were maintenance crew, Raj lost no time he immediately ran to the pilot and explained, "we need to rescue a child...she is on the roof..!" The pilot heard him out but shook his head, "who will lift her off.. I have no trained men...they have all been pressed into action beyond where the floods are raging..!"

"I know slither tactics I can do it!" Raj said.

The pilot did not seem to hear anything. He mumbled, "I am on standby-as soon as the weather clears I will be involved in rescue sorties. Moreover you need permission to take me off on a single mission."

As the pilot moved dismissively to leave, Raj stopped him. "Look rescuing a child is equally important. Just a matter of some time...please? Please just take this risk ... the location is just east of here-open space totally."

"Sir the rain winds....er...." The pilot was touched by the appeal. He stared up at the skies as if ascertaining something.

Raj spoke with earnestness, "See sometimes for a good cause you can break a rule...old chap!". Suddenly from behind Dumpu who had been stationed quietly on one side crept up and with some intelligence stared with the same earnestness at the pilot.

Self consciously the pilot gave a half grin then said "ok---er...maybe if I ...oh alright.... don't waste time---give me the location!"

Raj quickly did that.

The pilot nodded. Within seconds the helicopter took off; the rain proving to be a dangerous outcome of the weather for the intended mission. The battering rain drummed ominously over the machine. The pilot seemed to have a very keen and cool mind. He expertly guided the craft. Raj stood at the open entrance and peeped out to spot Tinku. "There-there she is down there!"

Raj shouted pointing to the broiling floods below. Yes, finally they reached the barn where Tinku clung on for dear life. The winds had started up. Aligning the helicopter for Raj to slither down and bring Tinku up was turning into an erroneous task. Wearing thick gloves Raj was poised at the entry of the copter. Winds buffeted the craft crazily. The pilot pulled up higher, then with a slight twist and tricky push at the stick managed to steady the helicopter over the barn. gnawwwwwwwwwwwwwwwwwwwwww--- crackcckckkck!"

The ominous sounds filled Tinku's head.

But things seemed to be turning from bad to worse. With one terrible crack the other side of the barn collapsed. Tinku tried to hold on but everything around her was collapsing. Water choked her throat and slammed her body mercilessly. She was tiring. Holding on or even paddling was becoming hard. "Oh I am so tired....I cannot hold on . She could only flay with her hands. "ohhhhhh I can't swim anymore....!" Tinku sighed. Like a flotsam on raging ocean Tinku was thrown up into the waters. She lifelessly buffeted crazily before going under.

Raj had trussed up the winch rope around himself when he was about to slide. He watched with horror as Tinku went down.

•••

"What happened?" Lito and Divya were greeted by a chorus when they entered the cheerful environs of the Mess. The Unit ladies immediately helped Divya to a chair. "Get some ice I think there is a sprain. And we could do with some coffee…!" Someone even rushed up with towels.

Divya was very sheepish. She was overwhelmed by the concern and helpfulness of the very ladies who she had constantly snubbed. When Lito placed the ice pack gently over the sprain Divya whispered, "I have behaved so badly…yet you came looking for me…?"

"Divya we are family…it was important we be together till our er heroes returned!'" Lito grinned.

Suddenly Divya in that one moment realized the enormity of what Lito had been trying to convey to her all along. Divya looked around. Everyone was together – there for each other. Even though it was scary and stormy outside they had created a haven here. That was what it was all about; her own immaturity to understand all this made Divya cringe with shame.

•••

With horror from above Raj and his comrades saw Tinku plunged and vanished into the waters. "Oh no she has gone!" The pilot yelled. "No wait.....!" Raj scanned the watery surfaces. His eyes caught something. Tinku was wedged between two uprooted tree logs that had anchored her some how. Since Tinku now was in the middle of the churning waters, even swimming to her was not a possibility. She was flowing forward fast and her location constantly shifting. If one viewed the place one would see the vast expanded swell of the flash floods enjoined into the existing tributary; miles and miles of rushing streams heavily flowing forward to join the main river. The danger that the influx of the pounding waters would soon dislodge the logs and carry Tinku away prevailed.

"Take the copter there –follow her!" Raj shouted against the wind and whine. He had been hauled back into the copter.

"Sir this is dangerous. Winds, rains make it highly dangerous for the machine....tell me you don't want to do this...find some other way...."

Raj thought for a moment. He looked out and assessed the subject of their discussion. Yes Tinku was stuck at a very hazardous location even aerially considered. Since she was being buoyed by the streams her location was shifting. To find the right moment to lift her off could prove vey dangerous. Notwithstanding the fact that the floods had created their own turbulence of currents in the merging tributaries waters, the intense foliage nudged within ranges also were proving to be a perilous! Tinku had unwittingly fallen into the most sensitive point of the merging waters. I cannot give up without trying-if I execute things quickly I can just manage to save her. Raj thought. With a determined look he answered the Pilot,

"I have to try. Give me just five minutes, *any danger we can* move away." Raj coaxed the pilot. Reluctantly the pilot complied.

"Tack tack tack!" The whine and propel of the copter blades drummed with some striking sequence! The rocking copter was dangerously aligned to the spot Raj pointed out. In preparation Raj had already jumped out and now dangled on the rope, high above. The helicopter found it difficult to remain steady. It jerked and shook dangerously. Raj crazily swung like a pendulum.

With some precision the copter, still having Raj balancing himself precariously, slide to position itself right. They raced towards the sailing forward Tinku. The copter managed to reach her.

Raj was just above Tinku now. "Tinku, Tinku grab my hand.....Tinku!" To his horror he realized Tinku had fainted due to the shock of the plunge. Raj in those split seconds took a risk he never would have normally.

Just imagine the scene. Tinku between the logs sailed swiftly forward-above Raj hung on a winch tried to catch her! Things worsened, since she kept moving!

Twining his leg into the green cloth strap attached to the steel rope winch he turned upside down and held on to the rope. "Thwackkkkk!" Winds hit Raj. His arm muscles ached as he maneuvered himself. Blood rushed to his temples and an intense pressure built up around his head since he was up side down. Rain droplets streamed down his face, irritating his nose. But Raj concentrated on his task only. Extending his hands he stretched. His intention? To physically grab Tinku. Raj stretched trying to reach her. Oh no she was swept further forward. Raj gritted his teeth as the pilot followed up. Now this actually was not how normally these rescues took place. Usually there would be a stretcher and more hands to help. But in this unique situation luck played along. The pilot after much trepidation, actually tilted the copter to bring Raj nearer to Tinku!

"Aaaaarghhhh!" Raj swung crazily. His vision blurred and teeth vibrated. Sweat, raindrops trickled into his eyes and nose. The pressure of being upside down was building. Raj schooled his mind to concentrate. He tried to keep Tinku with his sight.

He whispered "one ,two,,three" and with one lunge he yanked up Tinku.

Hanging upside down with the child fastened by the entangled rope on his ankle Raj flew away from the danger spot. "She has just fainted-I can feel her breathing!" Raj shouted to the no one in particular as he sailed the rainy skies holding on to his precious cargo. He had rescued Tinku.

17

"Sir I cannot believe you just did that!" The Pilot rushed up as Raj was untangled and Tinku covered up by blankets by the waiting soldiers at the helipad. The Pilot stared at him in absolute awe!

Raj grinned. He was sitting on the gravel un-strapping the winch and strap. Helpful hands had taken Tinku who was groaning awake.

"Sir? Are you listening? That was one of the most risky operations I have ever seen..."

Raj shrugged and grinned again not sure how to respond to so much of awe!

Raj finally free of the straps walked to the high and huge hangar like cover. He did not mind he was wet. Inside he walked up to Tinku who had been made comfortable on a make shift made in the hangar. She smiled weakly. "Tinku we shall wait for it to stop raining. Your parents are at the shelters the Army has provided for flood victims."

Tinku round eyed nodded. Leaving her to rest, Raj moved towards the entry. Rain drummed incessantly over the steel/ aluminum roof. Gratefully accepting the hot cup of coffee he stood and stared out. Suddenly he laughed out loud. Peeping inside from the side was Dumpu! "Oh I had forgotten about you!" Much to the fascination of all present, Raj led the elephant into the huge cover. Dumpu immediately stood over Tinku. She almost went hysterical meeting him.

•••

The next morning everyone woke up with the happy acknowledgement that the rain had stopped. And no earthquake had worsened the situation. Slowly people walked out from their shelter, homes and other place to view the damage. It was huge. The flash floods had all but drowned the Sen gardens. The paths from the hill point, winding down the Sen gardens and finishing after three villages was submerged in waters! Rescue and relief was provided by the civil authorities and the Army.

The army soldiers, worked tirelessly,

shoulder to shoulder, with the civil authorities to rescue victims in the subsequent days. Boats were piled into action. Food supplies were thrown in some inaccessible areas. Everyone was talking about the terrible flood. Sens had relocated to another garden on higher grounds. It would take some days before things would be normal again. All officers of Col Kher's unit had been up all night helping with the rescue operations. They continued their help in the following days too. Brave soldiers regardless of lurking dangers plunged into whirl pools, water holes and saved people. Food packets, water and supplies were generously distributed. The helicopter was pressed into action too. The unit ladies gathered together and began to give help whichever way they could. Clothes, food, water was generously contributed by every family.

One Month Later...

Divya picked up the phone and called Savitri.

"Hello! Divya here. I was just calling to ask if I could come along for the Plaster of Paris curio making classes conducted at the welfare center by Shivi?"

"Of course Divya...do come. We begin at 4 pm to 6 pm..."

Divya and Savitri spoke for the longest. Finally Divya put down the phone. Prakash entered and Divya grinned at him happily running to go to the kitchen to set his breakfast. "Hey Divya my leave is through.. you should be really happy since ever since we came here you have been clamoring to go home! So we leave tomorrow , you can stay with your parents for a..."

"Captain Prakash..leave? I don't want to go on leave..I am having too much of fun here...in fact leave we take later, lets plan a big party to thank the folks who set my thinking right...hmm Mexican food should do great as a menu....!"

Prakash smiled and shook his head in wonder. However he loved the change that had come over his wife...

"Reconstruction work and ..." Col Kher stopped as he heard a knock at his office door. His colleagues and he were in a meeting. An office worker entered and said tentatively, "sir there is a gentleman and er child who are insisting on meeting you." He added more clearly, "Mr Sen and his daughter...er Tinku want to meet you and er Major Raj."

Col Kher guffawed and boomed "Of course of course! Ha ha! Raj your fan club is here!" Raj grinned. Deb and Tinku entered.

Tinku ran to Raj and without any ado settled on his lap! Deb shook hands with everyone and then turned to Raj gratefully, "unbelievable work-you saved" his voice broke but he continued, "you saved my child, thank you....this entire month has been so chaotic...I could not come personally..you are such a good soldier-so determined and committed.....you did not give up...I er I do not know how to thank you..."

Raj lifted Tinku up and set her down he walked up to Deb and patted his back, "Deb it is alright....!" An awkward pause ensued since Raj too was very embarrassed by so much of praise! Then Deb said, "I have given up these gardens and moved up...these will become natural grazing grounds for the jungle animals. I plan to take care of -----plantation he took the name of a famous tea plantation whose owners stayed permanently abroad. "I love this life so relocation hereabout is my best solution."

"Dumpu comes along too...then Papa says there is a real school there and I will finally stop home schooling-oh but Mama should not mind I don't want hurt her by criticizing her home school...but...er!" Tinku suddenly stopped as she saw how her excited prattle had inspired amusement all around! Col Kher asked for coffee and cakes. Tinku was treated to a big bar of chocolate too.

•••

Later that evening Raj went for a jog. He observed flood hit areas and marveled at how fast the reconstruction was happening. He ran far ahead and suddenly found himself at an isolated spot. Raj stopped jogging and took a deep breath. The rich flora fauna around was so vivid that his senses could not absorb it all at once. Suddenly there was a crackle behind him. Raj froze. What was it? He could feel a presence behind him. Was it a militant? Trying not make a sudden moves Raj waited. If he attacks from the back I will take him down with a *tae kwon do* move...Raj alertly planned. He stood waiting. Waiting and more waiting. Gradually Raj decided to turn around and confront whoever he felt behind him. Raj very slowly rotated his body.

He stood stumped for a second, before bursting into loud chuckles. Dumpu was stationed right in front swaying and almost seeming like he was smiling. Raj chuckled and greeted him, "Dumpu you cannot sneak up behind me like that. You would have been treated to some *tae kwan do moves!!*"

Raj stroked Dumpu speaking softly. "Ok Dumpu I have to jog now so bye, see you later!" Raj resumed his run. Well Dumpu liked this *soldier*. He wanted to be his friend. Dumpu decided he wanted to jog with his friend too!

So Raj found a heavy elephant running alongside as he worked the tracks with his feet on his run......

THE END